From Herring To Eternity

Also by Delia Rosen

A BRISKET A CASKET

ONE FOOT IN THE GRAVY

A KILLER IN THE RYE

From Herring To Eternity

Delia Rosen

KENSINGTON PUBLISHING CORP.
http://www.kensingtonbooks.com

KENSINGTON BOOKS are published by

Kensington Publishing Corp.
119 West 40th Street
New York, NY 10018

All Kensington Titles, Imprints, and Distributed Lines are available at special quantity discounts for bulk purchases for sales promotions, premiums, fund-raising, and educational or institutional use. Special book excerpts or customized printings can also be created to fit specific needs. For details, write or phone the office of the Kensington special sales manager: Kensington Publishing Corp., 119 West 40th Street, New York, NY 10018, attn: Special Sales Department, Phone: 1-800-221-2647.

Kensington and the K logo Reg. U.S. Pat & TM Off.

ISBN-13: 978-0-7582-8199-9
ISBN-10: 0-7582-8199-4
First Kensington Mass Market Edition: August 2013

eISBN-13: 978-0-7582-8200-2
eISBN-10: 0-7582-8200-1
First Kensington Electronic Edition: August 2013

10 9 8 7 6 5 4 3 2 1

Printed in the United States of America

From Herring To Eternity

Chapter 1

A.J. strode into the deli kitchen, stopped, shuddered from her shoulders to her fingertips, then folded her arms and looked me square in my baby browns.

"I am *not* going back out there!"

I had been standing behind the long stainless steel table, scrambling eggs for Luke, who was filling in for my cook, Newt, when she entered. A.J. was the star of my waitstaff, the Pavlova of the serving tray. With just Raylene and Thom on the front lines during the breakfast rush, I couldn't afford to lose her.

"What's wrong?" I asked.

Her thin, lightly freckled face was taut with horror as she said, "That witch is here."

The ponytailed blonde was the poster child for southern gentility. When she used the term "witch" or anything that rhymed with it, I knew she meant it literally.

"Mad's here for breakfast?" I asked.

A.J. nodded.

That's odd, I thought. "Don't worry—I'll take care of it, A.J."

"Sorry, but her face—"

"I know."

"It even scares Thomasina."

"I understand. See to the other customers," I said as I finished scrambling the half-dozen eggs and handed the bowl to Luke.

Managing a restaurant is 10 percent stirring, 10 percent cutting, and 80 percent psychoanalysis and handholding.

"Breakfast, huh?" Luke said as he flipped extra-crispy slices of turkey bacon. "Should I stir-fry frog's eyes in hen's blood for the Chicken Wiccan Omelet?"

"Only if you plan to eat it," I told him.

"You're disgusting," A.J. said to him as she turned and went back into the dining room.

"Hey, Ozzy used to gnaw off bat heads!" the aspiring rocker shouted after her.

"I'm not sure the folks at the counter are interested," I said as I removed my apron and laid it on the table.

"Well, they should be," he said. "It's history, man. *History.*"

"Right. Cook, Luke, unless *you* want to be history."

"Haw!" he laughed.

He was right. God help my loyalty to Uncle Murray's staff. They had seen me through some tough days and a supersteep learning curve when I'd inherited Murray's Deli from my late uncle. I owed them all. And however challenging they could be, I liked them.

It was difficult to believe it had been three hundred sixty four days since I first came down here to run the place—I, Gwen Katz, an NYU-educated accountant, a New Yorker whose idea of making lunch was a snap-shut plastic container, tongs, and a salad bar. I had only been to Nashville a couple of times during the previous twenty years to visit my I-left-your-mother-to-figure-my-life-out father and his brother, and friends had urged me to sell the place. But I had just gotten out of a bum marriage, was tired of working at a brokerage firm that was under fire from Obama and from frightened investors—talk about DP, "Double Peril"—and at thirtysomething I decided to do something different.

I'd succeeded. Folks around here now referred to me as "Nash," short for "Nashville Katz," as though I was southern-born and raised on the pastrami game. In addition to learning the deli business—with the help and endless good will of my God-fearing hostess, Thomasina Jackson, who knew more about the place than I did—I'd also managed to be onhand for a couple of homicides.

I hadn't reached the point of wondering whether I was some kind of human GPS signal for the Grim Reaper, but it was a little freaky.

Speaking of freaky, that was the word which best described the lady who was sitting alone by the side window at the end of the counter. Her name was Mad Ozenne, the "Mad" being short for Madge. According to Thom, she was Creole on her father's side, Missourian Ozark on her mother's side, and living in Nashville because she had planned to marry a Cherokee jeweler named Jim Pinegoose. But the artisan had died just days before the wedding, suffering heart failure during a tribal competition dance at the Twentieth Annual Tennessee State Pow Wow in 2003.

"And just last week she tried to contact him through the tribal *atskili*," Thom had told me. "A witch. It was the talk of the church. Parishioners said they saw her and Sally Biglake in the woods behind Barbara Mandrell's home, incantationing."

"Why there?" I had asked.

"No one knows," Thom had said, inadvertently spookily.

"Maybe she likes the song 'Stand by Your Man,'" I'd suggested helpfully.

Now, here's what I meant about the attentive patience of my staff. Thom had looked at me sadly, took my hand in both of hers, and said, "Girl, that was Tammy Wynette. You want to take care not to make mistakes like that among the customers, 'less you want them laughing behind your Yankee back."

"Good advice," I had said. "And how should I take the—what did you call it? Incantationing?"

"Seriously," Thom had replied without a trace of sarcasm. "That stuff has some potent qualities."

The woodsy witchery was forgotten for more important business. The next day, Thom had given me a big stack of CDs. Within weeks, I was so immersed in country that I not only knew the lyrics to "Jambalaya," I knew what "Me gotta go pole the piroque" meant.

No longer a mistrusted Northerner, I beelined smiling through the "good mornings" of the diners to station number seven.

Mad Ozenne was in her early fifties, a tiny, bony woman whose long graying hair hung loose over her ears. She wore cotton crinkle skirts and caftans, typically with astrological patterns or crescent moons. The pagan attire wasn't the strangest thing about her, however. What had set A.J. off, and what drew stares from diners who did not know Mad, were the tattoos on her cheeks. She had all thirty-two teeth inked on the outside.

Sweet young Dani, who usually worked the afternoon shift—and was no stranger to piercings and body art—once asked, "Ma'am, forgive my askin', but didn't that *hurt*?"

"Very much," the woman had replied.

"Then why—?"

Mad had looked up at her and said, "The better to eat you with, my dear."

When she came for lunch, Mad always ordered chicken broth soup with a side of *gefilte* fish, heavy on the horseradish. I was frankly curious why she was here for breakfast and what she'd have. The woman was studying the menu, mouthing the words as though they were a runic conjuration.

"Good morning," I said pleasantly. "We don't usually see you here so early."

"I'm not an early riser," Mad agreed. "The dawn moon and Venus required it. The earth is not happy. I will have three raw eggs in a bowl with Hebrew salt on the side, and four slices of dry rye toast."

"You mean kosher salt," I clarified.

"The large crystals."

"Yes, that's kosher salt," I said. "You got it."

"It's very tasty," Mad said, opening and closing her mouth in anticipation and causing her ink teeth to move in an unnatural, sinuous fashion.

"I'll be right back," I smiled.

I was accustomed to patrons making innocent comments about "Hebrew" this and "Jew" that. I liked to believe it was uneducated shorthand, not malice. For nearly a year, though, I wished that some of these people were thrust suddenly and without preparation into Manhattan and faced the quick education I had had to endure down here. They wouldn't survive a week.

Mad watched me as I hurried off. As I passed the end of the counter on the way to the kitchen, Lippy Montgomery stopped humming—it was more like one of those soft, sibilant whistles where your tongue is pressed to the inside of your upper teeth. He swiveled and tugged at my sleeve. His round face, looking older than its late-twentysomething years, with its chronic hangdog expression, seemed more distressed than usual. He held the check in one hand; the other hand rested protectively on the battered trumpet case which sat on his lap, plump and frayed like a pet Pomeranian.

"Excuse me, Nash, but I don't think this check is right," the young man said.

"What's wrong?" I stepped around to glance at the bill.

"The herring platter, while uncommonly tasty, as was the grapefruit juice, is usually six ninety-five, not seven-fifty."

"The Russians are charging us more," I explained. "We're not making an extra red cent profit—if you'll pardon the pun."

Lippy looked at me blankly. He was not a political scientist; he was a horn-playing high school dropout who left Hawaii, he once told me, to seek fame in Music City. After all the years here, he was still performing at local bars, at funerals, and on street corners.

"We changed it on the menu," I added, reaching for one from the metal holder.

"I'm sorry," he said. "I didn't look at the menu. I always order the same thing." He looked pained. "I'm really tapped out," he said quietly, apologetically. "I've got enough for the old price and a small tip."

"I see," I said. "Not a problem." I took the pen from behind my ear, plucked the check from his bony fingers, leaned on the counter, and scratched the number out. "Old price for today. I also adjusted the tax down. When you pay, if Thom gives you a hard time, let me know."

"Whoa! You did that in your head?"

"Simple economics," I said. The Wall Streeter in me had skills that sometimes frightened the staff and clientele alike.

Lippy sighed. "Money isn't simple."

"No, but it makes the world go 'round, world go 'round," I Joel Greyed him—instantly regretting it, because now the song would be in my head for the next dozen hours or so.

"Money is necessary, but there are more important things," he said. "Like music. Like health."

"You can make yourself sick without money, and then you couldn't play," I said.

"I can always play," he said, caressing his trumpet case with a little smile.

It was time to move on. I sidestepped Raylene, who was coming around with coffee refills, then turned like a swinging door to make way for A.J., who was moving extra fast to make up for not waiting on the tattooed Wiccan, before finally making my way behind the counter to place Mad's order.

Luke snickered as he set a breakfast melt—egg, cheese, and corned beef on a roll—under the heat lamps and dinged the service bell twice for Raylene.

"That's kinda cool," he said, looking at the check. "Remember when Rocky had raw eggs for breakfast? Maybe that's where she got the idea."

"She doesn't strike me as the movie-going type," I said.

"Unless it's a brain-eating zombie movie," Raylene said as she picked up her order.

"She didn't order brains," I pointed out.

Raylene made a face. We didn't serve brains, but sweetbreads and tongue were both on the menu. They were two things she refused to serve. I didn't know this for certain, but I suspected I had the only waitstaff in the state that had the temperament of artistes. No one but my uncle Murray—and now me—would have tolerated it.

A man at the counter called my name. I turned. It was Robert Barron—"Robber" Barron, as the waitstaff called him. The six-foot-three former Marine was a treasure hunter who trawled through World War II naval graveyards, hunting for relics to sell online. These included dog tags of sailors who had gone down with their ships. His actions were protected under maritime rules of salvage and "prize laws," the recovery of booty resulting from conflict. He was very unpopular among veterans and with families who were forced to buy back the belongings of loved ones.

"Morning, Robert," I said politely, but no more.

"How are you, beautiful?" he asked, pulling little iPod buds from his ear.

"'How art thou, Romeo?'" I replied.

"What did you call me?"

"I wasn't calling you anything," I said. "It's a play on what you said . . . never mind."

"Yeah, my schooling in the classics isn't so great," he said. "But here's something for you. Did you know that witchcraft is a religion? Officially, I mean."

I shrugged. I thought of quoting *Macbeth* but decided not to.

"They're tax exempt and even protected against hate crimes," he said. "I learned that when I was diving off Hawk Channel, south of Key Biscayne, in waters claimed as sacred to local Santería practitioners. I sent 'em an offer of money and when that was turned down, I blasted out a few angry e-mails. I got quick reprimands from the U.S. Department of Justice's Community Relations Service *and* the Civil Rights Division."

"The law protects all kinds of folks," I said pointedly.

He nodded in agreement, my harpoon having

missed its target—a man who plundered the final resting places of pirates and American servicemen without distinction. He gathered up the bags of supplies he'd bought in town and got up to pay, rolling his tongue behind his upper and then lower lips for unchewed treasure.

"It sure do. That applies to voodoo, too," he said. "Practitioners can cut the throats of baby calves and let them bleed out without PETA being able to do a thing about it."

"That smoked brisket apple sausage you just ate was glatt kosher," I told him. "The animal was re-strained and bled before carving."

"Nashy, that wasn't a value judgment," he laughed. "I'm the last one to criticize you people. I've hauled tuna on deck and gutted 'em alive, ate fresh sushi while they were still wriggling. I was just sayin' is all, seein' as how you was talking to the witch."

"Make sure you come back when there's a ten percent discount for sharing," I said, moving away.

"You people and discounts," he replied, shaking his head. "Come and see me sometime. I'm at Oak Slope. I'll show you the river."

I didn't answer; it wouldn't have been Shake-speare that came from my mouth.

You people. That was another expression that rolled hard knuckles up and down my spinal column. I had to stop myself from turning back and hitting him with his own plate.

I reached the kitchen as he reached the cash register. I thanked my Hebrew God that Thomasina was working out front so I *could* walk away. Another few seconds and I would have reached over to the grill and hit him with a hot metal spatula.

Any hash browns you lick off your face are free, I thought as I played the scene out in my head.

Mad's toast popped and I took her order out to her.

"That man has a dark aura, bad juju," she said gravely.

I knew she meant j-u-j-u. "He's a charmer," I agreed.

"I'm a charmer," she said.

"I meant he's not very appealing."

"No."

I set her meal before her. She had not looked at me the entire time she was talking.

"That man is a reason the planet is cross," Mad said. She leaned forward to pick pinches of salt from the dish I'd brought. "Something must be done."

Mad's soft voice matched the strange, ethereal quality in her expression. If she weren't so fragile-looking, I might have considered her dangerous instead of eccentric.

"Is there anything else?" I asked.

"This is all very well, thank you."

I left the check. Mad was Thom's responsibility now.

The breakfast rush was waning. Returning to

the kitchen, I made sure that Luke had things under control—as much as the young man ever did—then went to my office.

My cubby, my sanctuary, was in the back of the deli. I shut the door and plopped into the swivel chair. So much of it was just the way my uncle had left it. His yellowing handwritten notes for firing up the fryer and dismantling and cleaning the slicer were still on the bulletin board. The old plastic photo cube with pictures of him and my father and me—as a little girl—still sat on the desk, next to the Coney Island pencil holder. In it were pens that celebrated the fifth anniversary of the deli.

The chair cushion still bore the impression of where my dad sat. The vinyl had split in front and I could see where he had picked at pieces of foam. I'm sure if I looked, I'd find them somewhere under the desk or behind the filing cabinet.

The only thing that was really mine here was the laptop. And the memories.

Most recently, there had been the discovery that my father had a mistress down here, Lydia Knight. The crazy lady was in prison now, but she had put a pair of scissors into my arm right here, in this little room. What Mad said Robert Barron had done to the earth? That's what Lydia had done to this office. She'd made it an unhappy place. If not for the quick action of her daughter Stacie, the stab would have done more than five stitches' worth of damage.

I looked around. "Oh, Uncle Murray—you're here less and less every day," I said wistfully.

No sooner had I sat down to go over the inventory than I got a call from Stacie, Lydia's daughter. She had come to work here briefly after her mother was arrested, but the memories of the confrontation got to her worse than they did me. Plus, there were other people Stacie didn't want to see again. She'd decided to relocate to Southern California with her fiancé, Scott, who was recovering from injuries suffered at the hands of bikers. I had leaned on one of my old Wall Street connections to get her a job as a teller.

"How's San Diego?" I asked.

"It's got a lot of ocean," she said. "I'm driving to work, looking at it now."

"Nice. I'm looking at a stapler."

"Then come out here! I'd love to show you around. Thomasina can run things for a few days."

"True, but cruel. My conscience would give me tics."

"You're strange."

"I know. How are Scott's relatives treating you?"

"Couldn't be nicer," she said. "They live about forty minutes from Mexico. I'm learning Spanish just by working at the bank."

"Just don't mistake dollars for pesos," I cautioned. "What are they worth, about eight cents?"

"Seven point three," she answered without hesitation. "I check the exchange rates while I'm having my coffee."

I smiled. This kid was going to be all right.

I was about to order potatoes—for some reason, our *latkes* had been selling like hotcakes—when there was a knock at the door.

"Yes?"

"Nash? We got a situation," Thom said.

Thom's mouth had the wide, rippling aspect of a volcanic caldera. If she were calling for backup, it had to be serious.

"What is it?" I asked.

"*It* is in the bathroom," she said. "*It* wants to see you when *it* gets out."

I went and opened the door, wondering what the hell could have gone haywire in—what, five minutes? Less? Thom was already charging back to the dining room. I followed quickly. As I did, I noticed Mad sitting at her table, wiping her egg bowl with toast. She was still looking ahead but raised her left hand, pointed her index finger toward me, and sketched an arc in the air, points downward.

An unsmiley face.

The earth is not happy.

There was a man en route from the bathroom.

He was about five-six, bald, African American, and wearing a thick, tan camel-hair coat. He stopped at the cash register where he immediately began drumming the little spoon on the bowl of mints. He carried a thin Italian leather briefcase, also tan. My guess: a lawyer.

"Who is that?" I asked.

She passed two halves of a business card over her shoulder. The first half of the card said:

ANDREW A.
ATTORNEY-AT

The second half said:

DICKSON III
-LAW

I put the card pieces in the back pocket of my jeans. "So, who is he?"

"The evictor," she hissed as we reached him.

He put down the mint spoon, offered his hand, and smiled. "Andy Dickson, and I'm hardly that."

"You're hardly *human*!" she snapped, fixing her dark eyes on him. "Someone needs eminent do-maining done? He's your hatchet man. You want some prehistoric bones that rightfully belong to my brother 'cause they're under his gas station? This Mayflower Man will relocate you."

That explained it. This was personal. "Why don't you take a break," I told her.

"No, I want to hear this," she said, her eyes still pinned to him like gun sights. "You ain't here to rip up the street for a new water main, are you?"

"May we speak in your office, Ms. Katz?" the attorney said.

"I'm not sure your coat will fit," Thom said.

"Out here is fine," I said. "Besides, I may need my advocate."

"As you wish," he said.

Oh, this was an "as you wish" visit, not a shrug and an "okay." That meant he was here to present me with a fait accompli. I had no idea what this was about, but I was ready. Hot, molten New York steel poured down my spinal column and hardened instantly.

"Actually, Ms. Jackson, you might find yourself in support of this project," he said as he removed a folder from the leather satchel.

"Anything you're for, I'm against."

"Ms. Katz, I do a lot of work for historic recovery enterprises, not just locally but nationally," he said. "You may be aware that I began discussions with your uncle two years ago regarding the possibility that his home on Bonerwood was atop a suspected historical site of what is called significant importance."

"That's news to me," I said.

"I see." He snapped the case shut but did not hand over the folder. "Perhaps you're familiar with our local historical landmark, Fort Negley?"

"I've been meaning to take the tour," I said truthfully. That was something my former beau, Detective Grant Daniels, had suggested. It was about two miles from the center of Nashville; that was the entirety of what I knew about the place.

"The fort was built during the War Between the States, the largest inland fortification constructed during the war," he said with the practiced tone of a tour guide. "It was built in large part with the skilled hands and able backs of African American laborers. A diary discovered in 2003 suggests that these Nashvillians camped on what is now your property. Your uncle was alerted to that fact. He seemed quite pleased. At the recent Thirty-second Nashville Conference on African American History, sponsored by the Metropolitan Historical Commission and Tennessee State University, papers were presented with new research to support this claim. As a result, the Metropolitan Development and Housing Agency has agreed to grant Professor Reynold Sterne access to your property."

"You're going to dig up my backyard?"

"No." He handed me the folder. "Your basement den."

My own eyeball crosshairs fixed on his nose. I didn't open the manila folder. I knew what it would contain: neatly filled-out forms, documents with embossed stamps and legal writing, letterhead with a curt, impersonal order supporting what I'd just been informed of.

"We're gonna fight this, you hamstringer," Thom said.

"You will find, among the documents, an agreement signed by Mr. Murray Katz agreeing to allow authorized personnel reasonable access to the property for a period of no longer than one year if the time should come that excavation was desirable."

"What a mouthful of marbles!" Thom barked.

"So you're saying this is a done deal?" I asked him. "No public hearing?"

"A citizens' forum was held on February seventh, 2010," Andrew said. "That was where Mr. Katz agreed to the terms of the document. He even provided floor plans to the home, if you care to look."

"There was nothing about this in Uncle Murray's papers," I said.

"*That* is between you and Mr. Dag Stoltenberg, who I believe is represented as the attorney-of-record in the relevant line of the appropriate form."

"You say a lot to say nothing," Thom brooded.

I started going through the papers.

"I warned your uncle he needed a full-time lawyer, not a semiretired one," Thom went on.

"It wouldn't have altered anything," Andrew pointed out.

"Lawsy, I'm gonna alter *you*," she said. "You let them take my baby brother's fillin' station!"

"Voice down, please," I said. I didn't need to lose customers along with my den.

"Ms. Jackson—until two years ago, only five dinosaur bones had been discovered in all of Tennessee. Three tail bones, a foot bone, and a lower leg bone. The hadrosaurs found under your brother's concrete slab increased that number fourfold. And your brother got a fair price for his property, not to mention the attorney general agreeing to drop the investigation into price gouging—"

"Ralph was no gouger, you rat!" Thom said. "*He* was being overcharged and he passed that cost along!"

"Sadly, his costs were not the consumers' problem," Andrew said.

"Sorry to interrupt," I interrupted, "but there isn't anything in here that says I have to sell or relocate. Only that I have to provide access."

"That's true," the attorney said. "However, you will note that structural integrity of the premises cannot be guaranteed due to drilling, so there is a stipend for you to move into a—"

"Not moving," I said.

"You're what?" he said.

"She said 'not moving.'" Thomasina folded her arms.

Andrew looked from one of the defiant women

to the other. "Very well. I'll inform TSU of your decision and let you know if they require an indemnification in the event that you are injured."

A customer came over to pay. Thom took it.

"I didn't see anything in those documents that required me to cover their asses," I told him.

"You will." Andrew looked at me with a benign smile. "You are new to Nashville, Ms. Katz. You may not understand the importance of the university *or* the African American community whose heritage they have embraced and protect. Let me advise you that those are voices you do not wish to have raised against you."

"I got an African American voice, too," Thom warned as the customer hurried away.

"It will echo sadly in an empty deli," the attorney said, looking around. "That is, if you are able to hear it over the pickets outside." His dark eyes stopped on me. "Be wise, Ms. Katz. This is not a battle you can win. And that's coming from a man who's giving up dozens of billable hours if you take his advice. You should appreciate that."

I didn't like that remark. "Why should *I* appreciate that?"

"Because you're a businesswoman," he said.

There had been nothing that even hinted of intolerance in my year down here. I told myself I was just being overly sensitive to this man. I hoped so.

"Perry Mason, you want takeout?" Thom asked.

"Thank you, no. I've already—"

"Then why're you still here?"

The man smiled sweetly at her. He looked at me, still smiling, then turned and left.

"God help me, that man fills my good soul with evil purpose," Thom said.

"It comes with his job description," I said.

"What're you gonna do?" Thom asked.

I thought for a moment. "Give this Professor Sterne a call, I think. First, though, I have something to do."

"What's that?"

I replied, "Order potatoes."

Chapter 2

I hate to say this, but I wasn't really attached to my home. Not in the way that one should be.

I'd lived in apartments my entire life, and a couple of personalized rooms off a common hallway never got to be more than a place to hang my handbag. It's different for the *bubbes* and *zaydes* who lived in the same Brooklyn or Queens apartments their entire lives, with the same neighbors they'd always had. Homes are built by memories. When you live in a big city and don't spend a lot of time at home, the city itself tends to be your home. So the prospect of having the finished basement of my uncle's half-century-old house disrupted during the daytime—when I wasn't there—didn't exactly rock my rowboat. I wasn't even concerned about ownership, since what would I do with old glass bottles and discarded poultry bones except turn them over to a museum or historical society anyway?

But the steamroller nature of the thing ticked me off. You don't come up to a person you never met and give them an edict followed by a threat followed by a possible insult. I planned to raise a stink about *that*, maybe cost Mr. Dickson some future billable hours.

I ordered my potatoes from Chris Hunter, the Veg-o-Tater, an organic vendor who sold primarily to the growing vegan community and abhorred, with a flaming passion, the kind of greasy foods I serve.

"I hate what you turn these spuds into," he said again—good-naturedly, but not.

"You might as well just have that printed on my invoices," I said.

"It's not just you," he said. "Most of the city entombs flavor in clouds of boiling oil."

"Canola oil," I pointed out. "My grandmother used to use lard."

He shuddered audibly and hung up.

I was about to get the university's telephone number online when I heard noise from the dining room. There were shouts, tables and chairs scraping, dishes and silverware banging.

"What is this, *tsimes* day?"

Mad's comment about the unhappy planet echoed in my brain.

The commotion out front couldn't be Homeless Elijah. He always smelled very ripe and was occasionally belligerent, depending on what he'd been drinking, but he always came to the back door for handouts. I guessed it was either a mouse or Andrew had come back and Thom was beating him to death. I hurried out.

Thom, A.J., and Raylene were in the open doorway and a small crowd was looking down the street. At least the uproar wasn't about anything happening in the restaurant. Thom turned before I got there. She had an eerie sensitivity about movement in the restaurant, almost like she was a Lutz in Amityville.

"Someone said Karen Kerr got into a fight with Lippy Montgomery," she said.

"K-Two?" I said. "The mountain-size mixed martial arts fighter who has horseradish with everything?"

A.J. nodded. "She's one deadly beyatch. I've seen her compete."

"You have?" I said.

"My daughter wanted to go so I took her," A.J. said.

"Why would anyone want to fight with Lippy?" Thom said. "He's a pussycat."

"I've got pussycats," I said. "I kick them just because."

Thom looked at me crossly.

"Kidding," I said.

A.J. was standing on her tiptoes, trying to see.

"Too many people in the way—can't tell what's going on," she said as she went back to work at the counter.

"Well, whatever happened, it doesn't concern us," I pointed out as a pair of sirens converged on the street.

"Nash, this is *our* community," Raylene said portentously. "Everything should concern us."

"You're just nosey," I said.

"That, too," she admitted.

As I turned to go back to the office, I heard someone in the street shout, "My God, he's dead!"

That sent Raylene and Thom out into the street. I hesitated, not because I planned to join them, but, because—if it were true—that's what you do when someone you know dies. You pause and reflect on who they were and try again, in vain, to grasp the elusive reality of "here one second, gone the next." Lippy was a weird egg but a good one.

I noticed, then, that Mad was still there. The table had been cleared and she was just sitting, staring. It wasn't as if she were in a self-induced trance, because she moved a finger and blinked and smiled now and then. It was more like she was watching a movie play out in her head.

And then she turned—not toward me, but to the door. I followed her gaze and a moment later, someone entered. It was a woman I had never seen, about three hundred pounds worth, with puffy green hair and a pair of wide-open eyes tattooed on her temples and on her left eye. She wore a patch over her right eye and was wearing a long, black skirt with purple moon symbols and a matching cotton cloak. This was not a woman who went anywhere anonymously.

She came through the restaurant like a slow-moving squall, oblivious to the unoccupied tables she nudged aside by her passage. She pulled back the seat across from Mad, sat, turned toward A.J., and raised her hand.

A.J. was behind the counter filling sugar containers. She looked at me. It wasn't an imploring look, it was a "this is yours, honey" look.

I went over with pen and pad at the ready.

"Raisin Bran, please, with extra raisins," the woman said before I had arrived. "And ham and eggs and coffee. White bread toast, extra butter on the side."

"Will that be all?" I asked.

I wasn't being facetious and hoped the woman didn't take it that way. I asked that of every customer.

She didn't seem to take the remark ironically. "Yes, thank you," she said with a little wink of her tattooed eye. Unlike someone who could wiggle their ears, this was a skill the woman had to have trained for. And not, I suspected, for secular showboating in public places.

The rest of my staff was coming back inside as I handed the order to Luke. Even he—who ate too much of every bad thing—scowled at this one. I stayed behind the counter to stack the clean coffee cups.

"It's true," Thom said gravely. "Lippy's dead, poor guy. K-Two has been taken into custody."

"I heard her tell the cops she didn't hit him hard enough to do killin' damage," Raylene said. "She said he blew his horn in her ear as she passed and she just reacted."

"Maybe he hit his head," Thom suggested—just as she turned and saw Mad's companion. "Ginnifer?"

The big woman looked over. "Thomasina?"

Thom hurried over and threw her arms around the upper half of the new arrival, who had made a heroic effort to stand but ultimately remained seated. "Ginnifer, *what* are you doing back in Nashville?"

"Oh, just call it an impulse," she said. "Visit with some friends. How have *you* been? Still at the same church?"

"Still at Baptist," Thom said, stepping back. "Nothing changes in my life."

"Be grateful for that," the big woman said.

"You still in Atlanta?" Thom asked. "With that—that fella?"

"Fred, the Luciferian? No, that was just a 'thing.' I've been in New Orleans for five years now."

"Great town! What do you do there?"

"I give all kinds of palm readings in the French Quarter."

"How many kinds are there?" Thom asked. "Like, for people and dogs and cats?"

"Just people, dear." Smiling sweetly, Ginnifer took Thom's left hand gently in her right and held it palm up. She turned with surprising grace and raised her thick left index finger. "There's chiromancy, which is the reading of lines," she said as she teasingly traced a delicate path along Thom's skin. Then she opened her own left hand and lightly grasped the sides of Thom's hand from above. "Next there's chirognomy, a divining form that uses the shape of the hand and fingers to see into the future. And, finally, I use dermatoglyphics, the study of fingerprints." She touched the tip of her index finger to Thom's own.

Thom snapped her hand back as though she'd been burned. It took a moment for her to recover her poise.

"I see," Thom said. "So—you make a living at that?"

"Lord yes," Ginnifer said. "Folks do things on vacation they would never spend money on at home. And then there are the devout locals. People walk past palmistry shops in Nashville every day. But in New Orleans, the city of mystery—it's very different there."

Bending, Thom gave her old acquaintance a

brief parting hug and returned to the cash register. Her eyes were a little bit wide and her mouth
was a lot open. Thomasina looked as though she'd
seen a g-g-ghost, as the old cartoon used to say.

"That was very strange," Thom whispered. "Almost
like she was trying to seduce me."

"I noticed. Who is she?"

"Ginnifer Boone," Thom said. She stood with
her back to the table, and not just to muffle our
conversation. I got the feeling she didn't want to
look back. "I've known her since elementary school.
Ginnifer was booted from our church eight, nine
years ago for selling spell-casting paraphernalia
on eBay. I was the only one who spoke up for her
at a meeting of the board of trustees. I said we
could only redeem her if she was a member of the
congregation, but they were afraid she'd pollute
the younger, impressionable members and ex-
pelled her."

"If she was a Wiccan, why was she even a
member of your church? That's some pretty heavy
Christianity you've got there."

"Her family's been devout since the eighteenth
century. Their roots go back to Kentucky and
Daniel Boone."

"You mean *the* Daniel Boone? 'Daniel Boone
was a man, yes a big man—'?"

"Stop right there. And, yes, the frontiersman.
Ginnifer was always a little odd and I think she
wanted to sever her relationship with the church

for a while. This was her way of doing it. It was also her way of coming out to her family as a Wiccan."

"How'd that go over."

"Poorly. That's why she moved to Atlanta to live with some devil worshiper."

"What happened to her eye?" I asked.

"I don't exactly know," Thom said. "There was a malpractice suit of some kind."

"Did you know she was friends with Mad?"

Thom shook her head. "I should've made the connection, though. Ginnifer got those eyeball tattoos right before she left. It's part of some local sect she belonged to—Mad, too, I guess. I never found out much about it."

"So you don't know if they're good witches or bad witches."

"Ain't no such thing as a good witch," Thom said. "It's all voodoo and black arts. The whole time I was standing there just now, I heard Jesus whispering in my ear, *Get thee from me Satan!*"

I didn't tell Thom I found *that* a little creepy, too. I also didn't argue about how there's bad in every religion, from the Inquisition to the jihad. I did wonder, though, whether Ginnifer being here was really as innocent as just coming for a visit. Mad was upset about the earth being out of whack. Maybe Ginnifer was here to try and help set things right—whatever that might entail.

Luke pinged that Ginnifer's order was ready. I took it to the table and left the check with a smile.

As I turned to go, Ginnifer grabbed my hand. I didn't wrench it away but gave her a look.

Before I could say anything, Ginnifer placed a business card in my hand and let me go. I looked down at the card. There was a cell phone number printed on it, but no name. Beneath, written with what looked like a fork tine dipped in dried ketchup, was a time: *7:30 p.m. from your office.*

"What's this?" I asked.

"Please call," Ginnifer said.

"Why?"

Mad said as she walked past, "The earth wishes it."

Chapter 3

I don't know what the earth wished, but I wasn't thrilled by the arrival of coral-lipped reporter Candy Sommerton and her news crew from WSMV Channel 4. She entered solo, her too-high heels clacking on the tiles. She strode in as I was headed back to the office.

"Ms. Katz!" she said, waving after me.

I stopped, sighed. The blonde and I hadn't had any contact since our altercation over the last murder that happened around here. That had ended with me destroying TV equipment, apologizing later, and writing a check for nearly two grand. Which was worth it.

"Hello, Candy," I said, turning slowly.

"Hi-hi. I understand that this was the last stop Lippy Montgomery made before his tragic demise."

"That's correct," I told her.

"Would you mind coming outside and telling us what he was like when he left here?"

"He was full," I replied.

Sommerton smiled sweetly and took a deep breath—a celebration of the power of twelve-weight thread, given the size of her chest and the tightness of the blazer which strained to stay buttoned. Talk about full.

"Yes, of course he was," she said. "But—would you just mind saying that on-camera? And also what he ate and what he may have said to you or the waitstaff." She looked around. "I'll put them all on TV."

"Candy, I really haven't time for this," I said. "I have to earn back the money I paid the last time we—spoke."

"Time is a so, so precious thing," she agreed. "But it would be good publicity for your deli."

"Actually, it would be good *bad* publicity," I said. "People would come to gawk. Again."

"And order," she added. "Food. Paying customers."

"Coffee," I corrected her. "Not worth it. So, sorry, Candy. I can't help you."

"Ms. Katz, you know—you really do want me as a friend."

"No," I said as I entered my office. "I don't."

"Your uncle was very cooperative!"

"Then light a *yahrtzeit* candle for him, because you've got *me* now."

I went back to my computer to get the phone number of Professor Sterne's office. As I looked it up, I tried not to think about the utter strangeness of the morning. Even by our *farmisht* standards, this was one morning for the scrapbook.

And through it all, I could not help thinking again about poor Lippy Montgomery. I was glad that what turned out to be his last meal was, at least, a happy experience. How had he described it?

Uncommonly tasty.

That was nice; poor guy.

There was a direct line to the archaeology department at the school, and I read up on Professor Sterne before I called. There was a photo beside his biography. He looked, in a word, self-impressed. He was about thirty-five, with long black hair over his ears, thick black eyebrows, square jaw, thin lips set in a half smile. He was wearing a purple turtleneck and tweedy blazer. He looked like the kind of confident, slightly standoff-ish but charming professor every female student fell for, from which a handful were selected and eventually discarded.

I should know. I had taken that short, dumb, tragic journey myself back at NYU with Professor Levey.

"Okay, Professor Sterne," I said as I called the number. "Let's see you sweet-talk me into not giving you a hard time."

I mentally reviewed the message I would leave on his voice mail. It was a pointless exercise since he picked up on the second ring.

"Ms. Katz," he said in a surprisingly high but pleasingly southern voice. "How odd! I was just about to call you!"

"And here I am," I said stupidly.

"I can't tell you how sorry I am this project came to your attention the way it did," he said. "That had to be quite a surprise."

"To hear that my finished basement is about to become the American Troy?" I said. "You might call that a little unforeseen. Why were you about to call?"

"There are insurance forms that indemnify the school against certain types of damage—"

"Wait—that indemnify *you?*"

"That's right," he said. "Some folks try to take advantage of a little jackhammering by claiming vibration damage to electrical circuits or pipes—"

"You're going to *jackhammer* my basement?"

"Ms. Katz, we have to, in order to penetrate the concrete slab. I'm sorry, but this was *all* discussed with your uncle. The room will be double-sealed in polyurethane sheets to contain the dust—"

"This is only during the day, right?" I asked.

"That will depend on the size of the volunteer staff, how many trenches we have to dig, and how many wooden supports we have to insert in those trenches to prevent them from collapsing."

"So this could go on round the clock," I said, dumbfounded.

"Which is one reason we urge impacted individuals to relocate," he said.

"You say that like leaving your home for a year is nothing!"

"It isn't nothing. But it *is* necessary."

"Like a *loch in kop*," I said.

"I'm sorry, a what?"

"A hole in my head."

"Ms. Katz, there is more than just the research at stake here," he said. "Lives and careers hang on it. The doctoral dissertation of one of my students, Kamala Moon, depends on completing this research."

"Your concern is touching," I said. "Are you *shtupping* her?"

"What?"

"You're not even bothered by any of this, are you?" I went on.

"Given the historical importance of the site and the relocation we are offering? Frankly, Ms. Katz, not very much."

I was willing to bet that if someone discovered a diary saying that my *bubbe* had camped here, they wouldn't bother moving a dog house.

"Listen," he said, "I didn't want to start our association this way—"

"We aren't 'associated.' I'm being bullied and manhandled."

"Fine. If you are, belligerence is only going to make it worse."

"How can it be worse? Patrol dogs? Land mines?"

"Be serious," he said.

"I'm *very* serious, Mr. Sterne—"

"Doctor."

It took me a moment. When the left-field word filtered through my anger, revealed itself to me, I literally came to a complete stop—verbally, emotionally, physically. That was all he had to do just then—interrupt my very important concern with something trivial and self-centered. When my momentary paralysis ended, I cracked down the phone. If I'd been on my cell phone, it would have been in at least two useless pieces.

I got up, because I didn't want to remain seated. I looked down at the man's photo-face, which was still up on the computer. I was calm now, as I said to that arrogant digger of long-lost latrines:

"The earth is not happy, *Doctor* Sterne, and neither am I." I looked at the ketchup-inscribed card lying on my desk, the one Ginnifer had given me.

I absolutely would be calling at seven-thirty. I went back to the dining room.

One of the last people I wanted to see just now, apart from *Dr.* Sterne, was Detective-no-snide-

emphasis Grant Daniels. But there he was, my
former lover, overdoing the "I'm here strictly on
business" thing by not asking for me. He was talking to Thom.

"What's up?" I said, strolling over, doing my own
version of the we're-platonic dance.

Our eyes met but neither of us greeted the
other by name. I thought first names would be a
little too informal and surnames would have been
too formal.

"I'm here about Mr. Montgomery," he said.
"There was a receipt in his pocket. He had breakfast here."

"Herring platter," I said. "What does that have
to do with what happened?"

"I don't know," Grant replied. "That's why this
part is called 'an investigation.'"

Ouch. There was the first I-was-dumped-by-you-
so-I'm-responding-with-sarcasm barb.

"Did he talk to anyone that either of you can
recall?" Grant went on.

"Lippy wasn't very sociable," Thom said. "His
music was his only real voice. Did you ever hear
him play?"

"Occasionally, in the street," Grant said. "Did
you notice anyone watching him?"

That got my attention. "Why? I heard someone
hit him—a random thing."

"I'll ask the questions," he said.

Ouch again. Barb two.

"I wasn't really paying attention," Thom said.

I just shook my head once. That was all he was getting from me: bobblehead.

"Did he seem unusually anxious?" Grant asked.

Thom shrugged. I shook my head once.

"Do you remember who else was here at the time?"

"It was breakfast rush," Thom said. "The usual crowd plus Mad Ozenne. The Wiccan."

Grant wrote the name in his notepad.

"Robert Barron, the hunky ex-Marine," I contributed.

Grant wrote that down, too. He did not react to my description and I was instantly sorry I gave it. I was taking the bullying of *Doctor* Sterne out on him.

"Did you notice anyone eyeballing the trumpet case or happen to see anyone with it after the incident?" Grant asked.

Ah. That was the reason for the third degree. Someone must have made off with it after the attack.

Thom shook her head.

"Lippy seemed very protective of it." I spoke softly, a little bit of a peace offering. "But then, he always did."

"So nothing different today?"

"No."

"Thanks," Grant said. That was for my thaw, not for the information.

"I saw the horn," Thom said. "When someone said, 'He's dead,' I went out and looked. It was still in his hand."

"It's the case I'm interested in," Grant said. "Did you see that?"

"I did not," she said.

"So this is a case case." I couldn't resist.

Thom made a face. Grant did not respond.

"Who waited on him?" Grant asked.

"A.J. had the counter. He sat there," I said, pointing. "Barron was on the right side, Nicolette Hopkins on the other. She's a mail carrier."

"Did he talk to anyone?"

"Me. We spoke when I adjusted the price of the platter, right before he left."

"What was wrong with the price?"

"He didn't realize it had gone up," I said. "I lowered it."

"I'd like to talk to A.J., if it's convenient."

"Sure," I told him.

A.J. was out back on a cigarette break. I went and got her. When she went inside, I followed part way, poured coffee, then stood outside, near the Dumpster, thinking—first, about Grant, and how I couldn't blame him for being annoyed at how abruptly I'd ended things. It wasn't anything about him, per se, it's just that we weren't exciting together. After a day of crime scenes, maybe that was good for him. After a day of knishes and farfel, that wasn't good for me. It was something I'd only noticed when I met the local slumlord, Stephen Hatfield. That man was rotten to the bone, but charismatic. I didn't want to date him, but I wanted him.

Then I thought about the trumpet case, probably because I didn't want to think about the damaged part of me that preferred a crooked bully over a decent cop. When Lippy did his street musician thing, he usually had the case open, at his feet, with a few bucks in it to show passersby that their contributions were welcome.

An opportunist would have just grabbed the cash, not the case, I thought. Unless they wanted a crime scene memento, maybe to sell on eBay. *Stupider things had been done,* I told myself, then looked around. *Like surrounding yourself with the smell of garbage and stale cigarettes instead of going out front.*

But I didn't want to be with anyone and I didn't want to go back to my office where I had to deal with the residue of my talk with Sterne. I sipped coffee and looked at a cornhusk that a bird must have pulled from the trash.

And then Grant came out the back door. He was wearing a plain blue off-the-rack blazer with khaki trousers. White shirt, yellow tie. He looked like what he was: a sweet guy without airs.

"That was pretty awkward in there," he said as he came toward me.

"A little," I smiled thinly.

"I didn't know whether I should come out—"

"I'm glad you did."

He smiled. "I just wanted to say that as long as people keep dying around you, I'm going to keep running into you."

I laughed a little. "It isn't me. The earth isn't happy."

He looked at me curiously. I explained what Mad had said, and added—by way of a kind of excuse for my crabbiness—what Sterne had done.

"Gee, I'm sorry to hear about that," Grant said. "The dig, I mean. I'm not sure I'd put much credence in what a witch has to say."

"Funny," I said, "she was a lot more real than that putz."

"You want me to look into zoning regulations for a loophole? They might be violating sound codes, EPA standards—"

"Thanks, but I need to handle this myself."

"Don't you have enough on your plate?"

I shrugged. "My great-uncle Oskar used to say that aggravation kept him from worrying about his health, which is how he lived to be ninety-three. Maybe I'll make it to one hundred."

Grant's mouth twisted. "I'm not sure about that reasoning, either."

"Why? What did 'peace in our time' get Neville Chamberlain except the Blitz?"

"So we have to stay in shape for war, is that what you're saying? Happiness isn't a better goal?"

"I'm a Jewish woman," I told him. "Even when the wine glass is full, we're afraid someone's going to knock it over."

"So you do it yourself, just in case."

"Maybe."

"But I've seen you happy," he said. "When you're busy in the deli—"

"That's just being distracted," I said.

"—or when you were trying to figure out what happened to Hoppy Hopewell and Joe Silvio."

I finished my coffee and looked at him. "Yeah. That was fun. It was challenging."

"So it's possible," he said. "Without a blitz happening."

I shrugged.

He pointed at my cup with his thumb. "Or without spilling a drop."

"A miracle," I said.

He shook his head. "I've got to get back to work." He looked behind him to make sure no one was eavesdropping. Then he stepped closer. "Yeah, Nash. Someone clocked Lippy. And he did hit his head on the sidewalk. But I saw the scalp wound. It wasn't a killer. I think something else happened to him."

"What?"

"That's for the medical examiner to determine," he said. "But A.J. said he came here three times a week, sometimes more. If you can think of anything else, let me know."

"I will."

"Thanks," he said.

"Thank *you*," I said. "For trusting me with that."

"I still think highly of you. Wait, scratch that—it sounded more formal than I meant—"

"I know what you meant," I said. "And I appreciate it."

I gave him a little smile as he left. I wish I could have thought of something else to say, but I didn't want to invite any kind of reboot of the relationship. Because I thought about him, too—and what I thought about him was why I had to move on.

Making sure I *hadn't* splashed any coffee on myself—he was right about that, dammit, upsetting my imperfectly reasoned justification for pessimism—I went back to help get ready for lunch . . .

. . . slipping on the cornhusk and dropping the mug, causing it to shatter.

Chapter 4

My wristwatch was like a talisman—bewitched, bothered, and tick-tick-ticking.

All through lunch and our rush-hour dinnertime I felt it calling me, half daring and half urging. I can't say I was or ever had been curious about witchery, but then I had never met anyone who practiced it. At least, not that I was aware of. There was something irresistible about the simple conviction of those two women. I wondered if there were other Wiccans in their coven or circle or whatever they called it.

I also wondered—and this part of it frightened me a little—if the women could or would say words or burn leaves or roll bones to help me against the archaeological dig. I didn't have strong religious convictions and I wasn't convinced I had a soul, as such, but I knew I wouldn't feel good celebrating Lucifer or some druidic moss-tree god.

I didn't even feel right skipping my semiannual trips to temple on Rosh Hashanah and Yom Kippur. It's called "fear of God" for a reason.

And yet . . .

I was looking forward to calling. I was feeling beaten by Sterne, irresolute in my handling of Grant—I was still letting him in, emotionally, when, aside from the detective part, I didn't really want him around—and weak because of my strange desire for Hatfield, who I was still thinking about after just one brief-and-only meeting. The map of Gwen Katz was one of lots of pathetically unempowered troughs and few peaks.

Maybe Grant was right about that part, I thought. *I keep waiting for next shoes to drop, collecting and comparing them, instead of getting out of the shoe store.* I suspected the Wiccans were in a very different place than that.

We closed at seven and I waited in the dining room, eating a small green salad, drinking coffee. I kept the lights off so passersby wouldn't notice me and wave. I wanted to be by myself, but, again, not in my office. I hadn't been back there, in fact, since the talk with Dr. Dig-Dug.

So, of course, who should come to the door but the doctor himself.

I knew him from his photo. He tried the handle, shielded his eyes on the side, and looked in. Still looking in, he knocked. He was not dressed as he was in the photo. He had on a denim shirt and jeans, not a tweedy blazer and turtleneck. He was taller than I expected, about six-three. He was wearing black Frye boots.

"Aw, hell."

I got up, unlocked the door, and stepped back. He pulled it open.

"Ms. Katz?"

I nodded. My elbows were on the cash register counter behind me. In my head, my arms were crossed.

"I'm Dr. Sterne," he said, offering his hand. His move was accompanied by a *whoosh* of Aramis. "Look, I wanted to say I was sorry about before."

I accepted the hand but otherwise didn't move.

"I also wanted to say I'm used to telling students what to do. Sometimes I forget how to comport myself in the real world."

Comport? I don't think I'd ever heard that word used in conversation.

"I know this whole thing is a surprise *and* a terrible inconvenience," he added, "and I should have been more sensitive to that."

"Well—thanks for all of that."

"Do you think you'll have time over the next few days to talk about this, maybe figure out something that works for us both?"

Us both? I felt bile rising again. This guy, who wanted to wreck my home and domestic life, should be finding a way to accommodate *me*. "When do you—" I weighed my next word as though my self-respect depended on it—hope? want? plan?

"Intend to start?" he said.

The bile had peaked and sat boiling in my throat. "Yeah. When do you *intend* to dig up my floor?" I was an idiot. Did I really expect him to be different than before? Once a *schmuck*, always a *schmuck*.

He was caught totally off guard by my outburst. "We're going to start in a week, when the grant money kicks in. Listen, I apparently don't know the right things to say to you—"

"I know. So don't say anything. Do you have a key? Let me guess, Uncle Murray gave you one. Will you be bringing your own toilet paper—your own Porta Potty?"

"Ms. Katz—"

"Just go," I said, walking toward him. "I have a Wiccan to call."

He braced his hands against the door jambs and stuck his foot forward as I went to close the door. "Mad Ozenne and her group?"

I stopped myself from pushing him out. "Yes, why?" The curious taste of hope, strength, and "I Am Woman" came in one yummy bite, replacing the bile.

"Are you affiliated with them?"

"I'm catering a ritual," I said.

"Seriously?"

"No."

"Be careful. They're lunatics!" he half said, half laughed.

"In what way?"

"They're trying to raise the spirits of the dead."

It was dark in the deli but not so dark that I couldn't see his expression, his eyes. They had certainty, not curiosity. "How does that make them lunatics?"

"Oh, come on."

"Really," I said. "The people whose campsite you want to dig up—how many of them believed in things like voodoo?"

"It was called vodoun," he said.

If he corrects me one more time—"Just answer," I said.

"Well, they weren't Christians. Slaves weren't allowed to worship, officially, as Christians—"

"So the final *Jeopardy* answer is?"

"A small percentage of American slaves were Muslims, but most followed—let me see—there were the Akan, Orisha, Las Reglas de Congo, Mami Wata, and other faiths."

"Any belief in zombies in there?"

"Of course, but—"

"Snake worship?"

"Some."

"Were those millions of souls lunatics?" I asked.

"No, but we don't take those beliefs seriously today!" he said.

"*You* don't, you mean. Some contemporary Africans do. Haitians? Creoles?"

"A relative few," he protested.

"I don't care if it's one old lady in Lafayette, Louisiana," I said. "I'm guessing you would show them more respect. A bunch of my Jewish friends back in New York are into Kabbalah, searching for a mystical connection between people and all of eternity. And don't Christians believe the dead will rise on Judgment Day? Should they be treated frivolously?"

"You've utterly bewildered the issue at hand," Sterne said. "The Wiccans worship men made of twigs and mix crushed beetles and tree sap—"

"Christians eat the body of Christ and revere a man made of plaster," I said. "I serve *kishkes*, fowl intestines stuffed with onion and fat. The truth is, you uplift some folks out of one side of your mouth and condescend toward different people from the other. And why? Because you don't personally approve?"

"History has judged them, not me."

"History written by bigoted intellectuals like you," I said. "Get out of here before I stab you with my receipt spike."

He snorted like a Great Dane, glared at me like I was a chew toy, and left.

I closed the door very, very gently. Not because I was afraid I'd slam it, but because I had managed to burn off a lot of frustration in one brief exchange—and, wonder of wonder, miracle of miracles, let it fly at the person who actually deserved it.

"Well, Gwen," I said, looking at my watch, "now you've got a call to make."

Able to go into my office without fear of the face that I left on my computer screen, I prayed to God—and to any voodoo deities who happened to be listening—that I was right.

That Mad wasn't as crazy as he believed.

Chapter 5

It was the dial six syndrome.

I sat in my office—having left Sterne up on the computer screen where it was easier to hate him—and quickly, easily punched in the first six numbers on the card I'd been given. Then I came to a hard stop.

I didn't hesitate because of anything Sterne had said about the whole witchery thing being baloney. I hesitated for the opposite reason. What if it wasn't? Did I really want my worldview changed by people who had anatomical drawings on their faces?

Do you want your worldview changed at all? I asked myself.

Coming down here was a wrench and dealing with the odd collection of customers was a daily challenge. Those were all generally positive experiences. My father's mistress, Grant, murders in

my alley . . . not so much. Now there was the dig
and I was about to play a scene from *Macbeth*. At
what point did my head, too crowded with change,
throw my usual sensible caution out the window of
a speeding car?

Now, if I made the call.

But the archaeology project really bothered me
and the witches really bothered Sterne. The enemy
of my enemy—

I punched the seventh number.

"Hello, Ms. Katz," the voice on the other end said.

It didn't sound like Mad or Ginnifer. "Hi," I answered. "I was told to call this number—to whom
am I speaking?"

"Sally Biglake, priestess of the Nashville Coven.
Thank you for phoning."

"A pleasure. What can I do for you, Priestess
Biglake?" I asked.

"Sally is fine," she said, instantly placing her way
above *Dr.* Sterne in my book. "Tell me," she said,
"have your dreams been troubled?"

"By . . . ?"

"Darkness," she replied. "Spiritual darkness."

Just those words made the conversation seem—
not quite scary, but a little nerve-rattling. I was
tired, I was alone, and I was a little emotionally
sapped. I felt as if talking to this woman put me
one LinkedIn connection away from the dead.
The clicks and groans of the pipes and equipment
seemed a little louder than usual. How long would

it be before I imagined I heard footsteps in the hallway, breathing nearby?

"I haven't had any unusual dreams lately," I said. "None that I can even remember, in fact."

"I am glad, because I believe you are at a vortex of spectral activity."

I didn't hear footsteps, but that sent a little tingle through my lower back. "What does that mean, exactly?"

"The energy around us is comprised of five elements," she explained. "Air, water, fire, earth, and spirit. When I cast healing spells for my tribe and for my sisters, it is necessary that these five elements be in harmony. For the past week or so, the ritual has done nothing but pull my own spirit to the left-hand path from the right. The meditation that is a part of my workings leaves me feeling bleak and unhappy rather than fulfilled."

"So this means—?"

"The spirit component of the pentangle, the five-sided star, is wandering, not at rest," Sally said. "The earth has shaken the resting bones of those who are physically near to us."

"What does that have to do with me?" I asked.

"I have gone around the city with one or more of my sisters, searching for the source of this disruption. We felt it coming strongly from the east when we did a tracking ritual at Radnor Lake. By circling the area in decreasing spirals, we believe we found the origin."

"My house," I said. "The campsite of the dead Civil War workers."

"Not just a campsite," Sally said. "Human remains must be in danger for the earth to send them forth."

"Oh, great. My house was built on an ancient burial ground?"

"Cemeteries are consecrated," she said. "The souls cannot escape."

"Even better," I said. "My house was built on a mass grave."

"Again, no," she said. "The spiritual activity suggests that no prayers were ever uttered, that murders were committed and bodies disposed of without ceremony. Something has caused those souls to stir."

"Why now? Why not when the house was built?"

"That did not intrude," she said. "Something has communicated evil purpose to the earth."

"Like digging there?" I said.

"That is what we believe," Sally said. "Madge heard your conversation with the attorney. She believes that irreparable harm will come from disinterring any artifacts."

"Good luck with stopping it," I said. "Tell me, Sally. You said this has been going on for a week or so. How did the earth know before I did?"

"Scientists say that all living things have racial memory, but it is not purely genetic," Sally said. "Objects that were once alive, like the leather binding of a book or journal, retain the spiritual imprint of any life that has come into contact with it. It is like—I guess you could call it an alarm clock. Something like that has been much in use."

"There was a diary discovered in 2003," I said.

"That could very well be the conduit," Sally told me.

Remarkably, it never occurred to me that this was a put-on. It wasn't just because the woman sounded sincere. Crazy people could do that. It was what Thom had told me earlier: *"That stuff has some potent qualities."* It didn't mean I believed that my house was hosting a for-real Halloween. But when two very different people say the same thing, attention should be paid. It was like Murray once said about having a colonoscopy before he was fifty: *"What could it hurt?"* Besides, I had an idea.

"Sally, are you saying you want access to my property?"

"I think it is essential that we hold a Sabbat on the site."

"Is that like a Sabbath service in temple? Not that you would necessarily know—"

"Though the prayers I would imagine are different, our word comes from your Hebrew *shabbāth*," she said.

"Oh," I said proudly. My people had contributed something important to another reviled minority. "Would it be necessary for you to sanctify the ground in some way to perform this service?"

"Very necessary," Sally said.

"In that case, we are in business," I told her, thinking back to what Robert Barron had said about witchcraft being a religion. "What do I have to do?"

"Will you be home tomorrow night?"

"What time?"

"Midnight," she said.

"I don't expect I'll have a conflict."

"It is the first night of the new moon," she said. "That is the best time to communicate with the spirits."

"Is there anything I need to do before then?"

"No," she said. "Just don't let anyone further desecrate the grounds before then."

"You can be sure of that," I promised. "One more question, Sally—why did Ginnifer want me to call from my office?"

"The spirits may have interfered with your cell phone reception," she said. "They are energy. They do that without meaning to."

"Oh," I said. "Is that the worst they can do?"

"Yes," Sally said, adding ominously, "as long as their remains are not disturbed."

Chapter 6

Despite my chat with Sally and some trepidation before I got into bed, I slept soundly.

My cats, however, did not.

Southpaw and Mr. Wiggles had moved with me from New York. My steadfast companions after the divorce, they were named, nostalgically, for two of the happier times I remembered in my life: making it onto a formerly all-boys Little League team as a pitcher when I was eight; and getting an A+ on a sixth-grade science project that was a triumph of will over disgust—getting worms to reproduce.

The cats had been a little skittish for weeks after the move. That was not exactly a surprise; the sounds of Bonerwood Drive in Nashville were very different from the sounds of New York City. Which is not a knock against my hometown;

Nashville has fewer sirens, car alarms, and low-flying helicopters, but my borderline-rustic neighborhood has chainsaws, cars being repaired to the sound of vintage boom boxes, and the occasional what-the-hell discharge of a firearm. The cats also didn't seem to like southern litter so much at first, preferring the Japanese rock garden that was a going away present from one of my coworkers.

So while the ghosts, if there were any, didn't make their way into my dreams, I woke to find my cats not on the "man side" of my bed, where they usually flopped, but under it with my slippers and a colony of dust bunnies.

I'm not one of those people who talks to her pets. I didn't ask them anything like, "What are you doing down there?" or "You joining me in the steamy bathroom for my shower?" I would open the cat food and put it in their bowls, and they'd either come out or not.

Still, it *was* curious. And I did notice something else unusual; the warbler symphony that usually welcomed a sunny day was missing.

Either there are ghosts, we've got an earthquake coming, or a relatively exotic creature like a red fox or armadillo went rooting through the trash, I thought. I was betting on the pests.

I was out of the house by six, as I am most days. I parked in my reserved spot at the public garage—Randy, the parking attendant, kept it blocked with an orange traffic cone—then rounded the corner and walked past the Arcade, an alley lined with cafés, shops, and salons.

When I arrived at the deli, Newt was already at work, turning on the burners and reassembling the slicer, which gets broken down and thoroughly cleaned every night. I ate a banana and put on the coffee. Thom arrived two minutes after I did.

"You're here early," she said.

"Yeah—the ghosts let me sleep."

She shot me a look. "Girl? Ghosts?"

I told her not to worry and I explained about the night before. She shook her head, kissed the cross she wore, said she had every right and reason to worry, and went to work while muttering to Jesus.

A woman I did not know rapped on the door five minutes after that, while Thom was setting up the cash register. I was behind the counter wiping food from the menus.

"We're not open," Thom shouted.

I heard a muffled, "Is the owner in? I must see her."

"About what?" Thom asked.

"My brother," she said. "Lippy Montgomery."

Thom looked back at me. I was already on my way to the front of the diner. I turned the lock and opened the door for her.

Except for the obvious grief in her bloodshot eyes and the downturn of her mouth, the woman bore a more-than-passing resemblance to her late brother. She stood about five-six, had the same round face and big blue eyes, but her skin still bore the healthy color of the Hawaiian sun; Lippy's flesh had been burned to leather from years of playing outside. Her dyed, platinum blond hair was pulled in a pigtail and bright red lipstick drew attention to her pouty, bee-stung lips. She seemed to be older than Lippy, perhaps in her early thirties, and reminded me of one of those girls I'd seen in the Bunny Ranch show on cable. Not that I spent a lot of time watching shows about hookers, but after the divorce, I sometimes found it distracting to live vicariously.

"I'm Gwen Katz," I said, offering my hand. "My condolences. We're going to miss your brother around here."

"We're gonna miss his music, too," she said. "That boy could play the horn."

"This is Thomasina Jackson, my manager," I said.

"Hi," the young woman said to us both. "I'm Tippi Montgomery."

I knew, just from the way she said her name with an ever so faint accent on the last syllable, that it was spelled Tippi-with-an-i.

"Come on in, sit down," I said. "Would you like coffee?"

"I would love a cup," she said.

She came in and sat at the counter. She was

dressed in a black jacket and skirt, matching shoes and shoulder bag. She did not have any luggage.

"Where did you come from, Tippi?" I asked as I poured us each a cup.

"Atlanta," she said. "I left around one o'clock this morning. Drove straight through."

"Do you have a place to stay?" I asked.

"No—and if that was an offer, thank you. But I have to be back in Atlanta by tonight. Work."

"What do you do?" I asked.

She said frankly, "I'm an escort."

I saw Thom scowl. I thought back quickly to make sure I hadn't had any bad thoughts about the Bunny Ranch hookers. I hadn't. Having grown up with a hypercritical father and having endured a hypercritical husband, I was sensitive not to judge others. Even in my own head.

"So, Tippi, do you have—appointments tonight?" I asked smoothly.

She nodded. "I came to make arrangements for Lippy to come home as soon as"—she stopped, choked—"as soon as the coroner will allow. They're investigating to see whether he . . . whether it was the knock on his head that . . ."

"I understand," I said consolingly.

"I had to be here to sign papers, gather his belongings."

I put my hand on hers. She grasped my fingers.

I felt a little uncomfortable, hoping she'd washed after ending her workday.

"Well, what can I do for you?" I asked.

"The police told me that my brother's trumpet case was stolen," she said. "The detective mentioned that this was the last place anyone could remember for sure having seen it. I was wondering, hoping, that maybe he left it in the bathroom or under a chair."

"I saw him with it when I gave him his check—Thom?" I asked, looking past the young woman.

"He had it when he left here," she said. "He put it next to the register when he paid, took it with him when he left."

"Apart from the sentimental value, is there a reason you want it?" I asked.

"I think there must be," she said.

"I don't understand."

"What I mean is, Lippy and I e-mailed every day, whenever he took a break and went to the library, and he said he had something exciting to tell me about, something that was in the case."

"You have any idea what it was?" I asked.

"He said, 'It's a real treasure, sis. You won't believe it.'"

"Did he mean that literally?"

"I don't know," she said.

"Sorry, I shouldn't be pressing you. Just curious."

"It's all right," Tippi said. "If I'd thought it was

important, I would have pressed him. Lippy liked his surprises."

"I assume you told the detective about it?" I asked.

She nodded. "When I returned his call, he asked if I could think of any reason someone might want to steal it. That was the only thing I could think of. It's not like the horn itself was valuable."

"How long did your brother own that trumpet?"

"Since he left home. He bought it at a pawn shop in Oahu, one that sold mostly sailing mementoes—things retiring or needy old sailors no longer needed, like telescopes, charts, anchors."

"People hock anchors?"

"Not their own, of course, but from salvage operations," she said. "As you might imagine, many, many artifacts from World War Two have been retrieved in the Pacific Ocean."

"Of course," I said. I was trying to imagine how people got rusty anchors to shore—though I suppose if you could raise them from many fathoms deep, where they weren't especially buoyant, the rest of the trip was more of the same. The mention of salvage operations made me think of something, which I kept to myself. "So—you were saying about Lippy?"

"Yes, Lippy learned to play the horn in elementary school," she said. "He continued through the eleventh grade. That was all he lived for, he loved it so. During the week, he would wake us to reveille. My dad, an old navy man, was very proud. When he decided to go to New Orleans, Lippy tried to take the one that belonged to the school, but they saw him trying to sneak it out in his gym bag."

"Yeah, the shape would be a little distinctive," I said. "Wait—New Orleans?"

"He wanted more than anything to play Dixieland Jazz, but he stopped here first. He said he just planned to check out the music scene for a week or two—then fell in love with Nashville and so he stayed."

And that was the short, sad, sweetish story of Lippy—née Clifford, I learned from his sister— Montgomery. Her name really was Tippi, though, named after the star of her mother's favorite movie, *The Birds*. She had left Oahu after her mother's death. Her father had predeceased her and the mother's long illness left them with no money. Tippi spent some time with her brother in Nashville before answering a newspaper ad to appear in films in Los Angeles; after attending an adult film awards ceremony in Atlanta, she had decided that being an escort there was preferable to making porn in the San Fernando Valley. She said her brother came west to help her move. The drive back to Atlanta was one of their fondest times together.

We finished our conversation as Tippi finished

her second cup of coffee and a toasted bagel. When she left—with a couple of crullers and a refill of her coffee in a "to go" cup—Thom was filling napkin holders. My churchgoing manager was still scowling.

"Did you hear, Nash? Did you *see*? That girl was not even ashamed to tell us how she earned her living!"

"At least she's not on the dole," I said.

"You're defending her?"

"I'm not condemning her," I said. "Didn't you ever wonder how Lippy survived, even with as little as he had? Why he ordered the least expensive item on the menu? Why he haggled over the price with me?"

"I figured he made do," she said. "Dollars and coins in his trumpet case, a few weddings and such."

I nodded toward the front door. "That's how he survived," I said. "She sent him money. She had to. She makes her way in life, no apologies. I admire that."

Thom looked at me with a clergyman's worried eyes set in the big, unhappy frown of a circus clown. "Lady, you are consortin' with witches and praisin' hookers. I just don't know."

"It takes all kinds to make a world," I said. "Judge not, lest ye be judged."

"Go and sin no more," she replied.

"Get thee forth—," I started, thinking I had

something but didn't. "Well, it's another day in the neighborhood," I said.

Shaking her head, Thom opened the door for our first paying customers.

One of them was not Detective Grant Daniels. He came in; he just didn't order anything.

It was just starting to get busy and I was helping shred hash browns in the kitchen. I invited him to talk while I peeled potatoes. He leaned against the butcher block table, his face turned toward me so Newt couldn't hear at the grill—with the overhead fan on, he couldn't hear much of anything—but Grant was a cautious one.

"I got the medical examiner's report this morning," he told me. "Lippy was poisoned."

I stopped peeling. My first thought wasn't for poor Lippy. It was that line of Lady Macbeth's when she learns that King Duncan has been murdered: *What, in our house?* Why else would Grant be telling me?

"Another investigation," I said sullenly.

"I'm sorry, Nash."

"You're sure it was my food? What about the horn?" I asked. "The mouthpiece—"

"The instrument itself tested clean," he said. "There was a trace of toxin but that was on the mouthpiece, in Lippy's saliva."

"What kind of toxin?" I asked, with a sick feeling, thinking of what Lippy had eaten.

"Mercury," he replied. "Anita Fong Chan of the

health department is on her way to confiscate your herring. I used a little influence, convinced her to come around back so as not to alarm diners. You're going to have to meet her here. And take the herring off the menu, obviously."

"Of course." Fortunately, that wasn't one of my big sellers. "Can't mercury be inhaled?" I asked. "Wasn't that a problem in some factory a couple of years—"

"It showed up in the gastrointestinal tract, not the lungs. It was in the undigested pieces in his stomach."

Crap, I thought. "So we're talking a mega-helping rather than cumulative?"

"Yes and no," Grant said. "Because Lippy ate a lot of seafood—most of which he caught himself on the Cumberland River—the ME said his mercury levels would already have been seriously elevated. All it took was one big hit to put him over."

"Someone might have known that, right?" I said. "Lippy could have been targeted for some reason. It wasn't necessarily bad when we served it."

"Possibly—"

"Who even *uses* mercury?" I asked. "Thermometer makers?"

"Dentists, lab researchers, any number of manufacturers," he said. "It's used in antiseptics, switches, light bulbs—but anyone can buy it. Which is why— if you're done interrogating me—"

"Sorry," I said.

"I expected it," he said. "But that's why I need a list of everyone you or the staff can remember around Lippy yesterday as well as anyone else who ordered the herring since this shipment arrived. We need to test those individuals, rule out an accidental dosing of several people *or* a serial killer."

"Grant, it was breakfast rush. We were busy. Also, we write our checks out the old-fashioned way, on a green pad, and a quarter of our customers pay cash—"

"I know. Match them as best you can and get me the receipts. I'll have a court order for them by ten, just to keep the paperwork in order. Oh, and—does the herring arrive prepared or just as fish?"

"I don't sell Mc*Gehakte*."

Grant was confused.

"This isn't McDonald's. Nothing comes pre-chopped or premade. It arrives as semifrozen fish, on ice, in cardboard boxes lined with wax paper. I do all the work and mercury definitely is not an ingredient. I've never even seen the stuff, except in those old games where you had to maneuver the little silver blob through a maze."

Grant—who hadn't recovered from the McDonald's crack—looked at me as if I'd just described an alien abduction.

"The answer is no." I got back on point. "I'm the one and only middleman between fish and plate."

"All right. I'll want a statement about your prep procedures. I can get that later."

I nodded, thanked him. "Lippy said the herring was 'uncommonly tasty,'" I told him. "Would he have said that if it was poisoned?"

"I'm told that mercury doesn't really have a taste," Grant said. "He might not have noticed."

"But it has a consistency," I said. "I drain the oil when I cut the fish—he might have noticed it was greasier."

"Unfortunately, we can't ask him," Grant said. "And since *I'm* not a fish eater, I wouldn't know about that." Grant held my eyes for a moment longer with a you-remember-that-don't-you? look.

He was right. When we'd ordered pizza in, I had to pick his anchovies off.

Grant told me to do nothing on my own, no tasting or repackaging, just point the health inspector in the direction of the herring and let her retrieve and remove it. She would have to check the surrounding area of the industrial-size refrigerator, above and below the plastic container, for contamination.

He left by the front door a few minutes before Anita Fong Chan arrived at the back. I had met her twice before on her semiannual visits. She was a petite woman with an air of authority that stopped just short of arrogance. She was someone that everyone in my business had to please, and please politely and thoroughly. Virtually every word from her mouth sounded like "open sesame."

I opened the door. Then it was, "Open the refrigerator, please." "Don't open the container." "Open the files from Fishy in Tennessee and give me the order." "Close the door behind me." She asked if the original fish packaging was still in the Dumpster. I told her it was not. She asked me to open *that* so she could see. We went out back and I raised the heavy lid. She stood on tiptoes and looked in. Satisfied, she left. The transfer of allthings herring lasted less than five minutes.

I went back inside and told Newt to holler if he really got backed up. I said I'd be in my office.

"I'm guessing there's something *fishy* going on," my young cook said from over the hissing grill.

I didn't bother responding. I just shut the door, opened the expanding brown folder marked for that week, and started pulling the credit card and order slips from the last three days. And, alone with my thoughts as I did the rote work, I got angry at myself again for ever having dated that thoughtful but empty trench coat.

Chapter 7

Something Tippi had said stayed with me as I stopped stapling receipts to checks long enough to help out with the breakfast rush. It was what Lippy had told her: *"It's a real treasure, sis."*

Lippy had bought the trumpet in a place where seafarers sold their used wares. What if the trumpet had belonged to a sailor? And what if that hypothetical sailor had left an equally hypothetical "something" in the case, like a deed or a rare document like William Bligh's map of Tahiti or even a treasure map? It was possible. And that would make Robert Barron, who dined next to Lippy at least on the day of the murder, a potential suspect.

There were a lot of hypotheticals in that hypothesis, along with: if Barron were guilty, couldn't he have megadosed Lippy somehow—in his water, for example—knowing that our salted, smoked, marinated, and creamed Baltic delicacy would be blamed? I checked online: mercury was water soluble. The water could have mixed the mercury into the fish once they both hit his stomach.

I'm sure the ME considered that, I told myself. And it might not matter much. The idea was to find out who could have given Lippy the fatal dose, whatever the medium.

Which brought me back to Barron. Sitting near him, Lippy had seemed unusually protective of the trumpet case. Was it because he was suspicious of Barron or because of the treasure Lippy had mentioned to his sister? Should I simply put him on the list for Grant or talk to him myself?

That thought brought back the taste of the banana I'd eaten. I'd put him on the list.

I wondered if the witches could help. Or are psychics the only cuckoo bloodhounds who chase killers using objects like a shoe or a Kleenex?

That's not fair, I told myself. Neither was another homicide involving my deli. Maybe it was time to draw some kind of imaginary line in the karmic sand. Like chicken soup, it couldn't hurt.

It wasn't until after lunch that I'd managed to talk to all the staff about who they could recall having seen around Lippy yesterday.

"Didn't we already do this?" A.J. complained. "I told Detective Daniels everything I could remember."

"Remember harder" was all I had to say.

I didn't tell her or anyone else the latest. I

didn't need more gawkers coming to a murder site the way they did when my bread delivery guy was butchered out back—or, worse, shunning the place because they were afraid of being poisoned.

With some arm and brain twisting, A.J., Raylene, Luke, Thom, and I came up with seven counter names. In addition to Robert Barron, we had mail carrier Nicolette Hopkins, bus driver Jackie and her auto mechanic girlfriend, Leigh—Thom was as uncomfortable with them holding hands as she was with women who had body parts tattooed on their faces—bank teller Edgar Ward, advertising executive Ron Plummer, who handled our very modest account, and the CEO of Cotton Saint Tunes, whose name was Fly Saucer. Today he was on his iPad, but Mr. Saucer usually played his iPod too loud and had to be asked to turn it down. It was my belief that he did that on purpose because he liked Raylene. He made it a kind of gag to write his number on things for her: a napkin, a place mat, her apron, his business card. In his defense, the lady was attractive and had zero musical ability; a music business exec could be sure she wasn't trying to get ahead by dating him. And, I guess, at some point, even some men get tired of a succession of one-nighters.

Some. Not all. Not *most.* But maybe Fly was one of them.

Unfortunately for Fly, she already had a beau: FM talk show host Michael Hunn, who I had heard but never met. I don't think Raylene was trying to keep him from us, it's just that his waking hours coincided with our sleep time. I lived in fear of the day my ace server opted to set her clock by his.

I added the staff to the list, myself included, not because I thought any of us would have poisoned Lippy, but I knew that if Grant asked—and he would—I'd be especially unhappy with him. I e-mailed the list to him so he wouldn't have to stop by. It wasn't just a courtesy; I wasn't entirely sure he had accepted the breakup and I didn't want to do anything that would allow him an opening, like a late in the day drive-by that included the phrase, "I haven't eaten yet—wanna grab something?"

Some days fly by, others drag; this one wriggled. I was fine one moment, distracted the next—by Lippy's death, by the still-evolving plan to turn my basement into a Wiccan temple, by customers who seemed unusually needy, and by snarling inside at Grant and Robert "You People" Barron. I knew they were just convenient targets for my general frustration, but I didn't care. They deserved it.

I was in my car and headed home at dusk on Nolensville Road when a motorcycle passed me, too fast and too close. Swinging in front of me, the back tire spit a cloud of dirt and pebbles at my windshield. Through the tawny haze, I saw it was a Yamaha, not a Harley, so I didn't feel my life was in danger as I jammed on the gas and headed after it. The biker, too, was a case of transference, but once again I didn't care. I needed to race something out of me and the Wild One was it.

The rider turned onto Edmondson, which happened to be the way I was going. We were both doing fifty as we passed Wentworth Caldwell Senior Park. The bike stayed close to the shoulder, spitting more sand and gravel back at me, so I was forced to keep my distance. It was a clever tactic, but doomed; they'd be pulling over somewhere, and I'd be pulling up behind them with a passenger's seat tire iron and glove compartment can of mace in my hands. A single lady, and a New Yorker, I never left home without protection.

God was with me as the bike turned onto Bonerwood. I knew the road, I knew the dips, I knew the turns. I knew when I could pull to the left and avoid the barrage. I closed the gap from three car lengths to one. My house was coming up on the left, but I was going to . . .

. . . pull right into the driveway, just after the Yamaha.

I was braking while the driver—a hefty woman with a leather jacket, leather pants, and long gray hair—was just pulling off her helmet.

"That was exhilarating!" she said, turning toward me as I got out. "I'm Sally Biglake."

"You're also a reckless driver," I said.

"Always," she agreed. "Either the gods are with you or they are not. If they are not, you can just as easily die walking to the mailbox as you can speeding on a motorcycle."

"I'm not sure statistics would bear you out," I said.

"They never do, which is why I ignore them," she said. "What are the chances that a Wiccan, a Native American, and a woman have anything approaching 'fair prospects' in this world?"

Her logic may have been as crooked as Bernie Madoff''s books, but her conclusion was on target. And, though I should have expected it, I was still surprised as I approached her and saw, tattooed on her neck, an extra set of ears, one on each side.

"Hi." She offered her hand.

It was big and powerful, like her features. She stood about five-foot-ten, with a big open face, wide brown eyes, and a large smile that caused her full cheeks to double in size outward. I put her at about fifty, though that might be high. Her dark skin, especially around the eyes, was deeply wrinkled from the sun, making her look healthy but older.

"It isn't the sun," she said.

That caused me to start. "What isn't?"

"You were looking at my eyes," she said. "Most people assume they're wrinkled because I'm out in the sun a lot. I'm not. I'm out in the moon a lot, which is what does it. Have you ever tried reading ritual texts by lunar light?"

"Not since I was a Brownie," I said.

"Squinting is required. A lot of it. Then there's the smoke from the ceremonial fires. That isn't very kind, either."

"I work the grill sometimes," I said. "I understand."

"Sisters." She smiled.

I wasn't quite ready to go there, though I had to admit she had a kind of self-effacing charm her colleagues lacked.

"Why are you here?" I asked. "I wasn't expecting you until midnight."

"I told you that's the best time to communicate with spirits," Sally said. "There's prep work."

She reached into her jacket pocket, popped a Marlboro in her mouth.

"If you're going to smoke—," I began.

"Outside, I know. Actually, it's only partly because I like it. I came early to walk the property, see what the smoke reveals."

She struck a wooden match on a stone set in her bracelet. "Lapis lazuli," she said, holding the blue stone toward me. "The gemstone wakens the third eye."

"Especially if you strike a match on it," I suggested.

"You're catching on." She winked.

I wasn't, but that, too, made a kind of crooked sense. She lit the cigarette. Her face looked a devilish red in the glow. Her eyes snapped to mine as if she knew what I was thinking—again. She just smiled around the cigarette.

"What does the smoke reveal?" I asked—partly to end the creepy silence.

"Shapes," she said. "I'll be walking around for several hours. I want to see if any of the dead have risen. You haven't heard or seen anything unusual, have you?"

"Not me, but my cats were hiding under the bed this morning."

"That's not a spirit presence," she said. "If it were, they would seek high ground, like a shelf or dresser. Why get closer to where they're interred?"

Again—logic, however I wanted to argue against it.

"Will you need a light or anything?" I asked.

She shook her head and held up the glowing tip of the cigarette. "This is all I require. I'll let you know if I find anything."

I left her to her business and went inside to feed the cats and make some split pea soup and ham. I was in the mood for pig and that was something I didn't get a lot of at the deli.

I could see my small backyard from the kitchen window, and it was strange to watch the little red glow moving through the dark like an evil Tinker Bell. The cigarette didn't remain in her mouth; it moved way up, down, sideways, trailing a hint of smoke. Then it would stop as she inhaled before moving around again.

I did some bookkeeping in the kitchen after

dinner, then answered e-mails on my laptop. I didn't stay in touch with a lot of old acquaintances from New York, but those I did, I was pretty diligent about. I followed that with a little research. Around nine-thirty, Sally rapped on the door and caused me to start. She hadn't found any ghosts yet, but she did want to use the bathroom. She left a lighted cigarette on the concrete stoop, but she might just as well have brought it in from the way her jacket and hair smelled. The cats ran from us as I showed her the way. When I came back to the kitchen, they were up on the counter, beside the sink—the highest spot they could jump. That was a little freaky.

I fell asleep in the den watching the news and was awakened by the sound of the back door opening and Sally calling in.

"Ms. Katz? We're all here—may we come in?"

"Yes, of course!" I shouted. "But call me Gwen."

I ran back, rubbing the remnants of sleep from my eyes, as Mad and Ginnifer came in with Sally and I was introduced to a fourth member of whom I had known nothing. She was a novice witch, a gorgeous young African woman from Kenya named Dalila Odinga. She was dressed in a black cotton cloak that reached to her ankles. She did not have any tattoos that I could see, but she wore two silver snake bracelets and a matching necklace.

"She practices Damballah voodoo and is new to America," Sally said. "She is a stockbroker."

"I used to be in finance, on Wall Street," I said. I did not crack-wise about "voodoo economics" but asked in earnest, "Do the spirits guide your investments?"

Dalila looked at me strangely. "Wouldn't that be rather reckless? No, I use the standard indicators, though my specialty is capitalizing on the weekend effect. I do my most profitable buying on Mondays when stocks open lower."

"Sound approach," I said, feeling a little silly. I looked at Sally. "So, how did it go out there?"

"Very well," she said. "I encountered only one spirit—and she was not from the campsite."

"She? Who was it?" I asked.

"I do not know," Sally said. "She was confused, as many new spirits are. She said she was a teepee."

Chapter 8

I excused myself and went to the den. It had to be a coincidence. Or a joke. Or something other than what I was thinking.

I went to where I'd left my cell phone to charge. There was a call from Grant Daniels—from earlier in the evening.

"Nash, call me," he said. "It's urgent."

I took the phone into the bedroom and closed the door. I called.

"Did something happen to Tippi Montgomery?" I blurted when he answered.

"She's dead," he said. "How did you know?"

"I was—it was a dream," I said. "That's why I didn't hear your call."

"Well then, you're psychic," he said. "A witness saw Tippi pulled into the parking lot of the Kroger on Monroe around one-fifteen. She was eating pastries, apparently having a cry. She drove off about a half-hour later. The NPD found her dead in her car at two-fifteen on Jefferson. The car just stopped in the westbound lane. They also found a coffee cup from Murray's and a half-eaten cruller."

"Poor girl," I said. The sentiment sounded trite, but I meant it. She'd died because she was devoted to her brother. After that sunk in, I replayed what Grant had said: she'd been eating crullers from my deli. "Aw, crap."

Grant knew my moods. "Yeah," he said. "I hate to do it, Nash, but—"

"You need my crullers, too."

"And coffeepot. Just in case."

"I drank from that, too, Grant. All day."

"I understand," he said. "But if the ME finds that she was poisoned—"

"Fine. Hey, maybe the killer has it in for me or the deli, not the Montgomery family," I suggested.

"I don't think so," Grant said. "Between us, whoever did this took Lippy's belongings that Tippi picked up from the coroner. We think he or she must have been in the car when Tippi pulled into Kroger and got out before she got to Jefferson, since someone would have seen the individual get out after that. There's not a lot of surveillance along the route she took."

"Do you think someone scoped out the area first?" I asked.

"Not necessarily. The security cameras aren't exactly difficult to spot," Grant said. "That's part of the deterrence factor. And who would have known which way she was going? No, the killer probably just asked her to pull over. If she was poisoned, maybe she was already feeling faint."

"What about her cell phone?"

"The killer left it. The last call made to her from this area was from me."

That was discreet of him: "from this area." No doubt she had calls from clients back in Atlanta.

"Grant, do you know what she did for a living?" I asked.

"Yes," he said solemnly. "She had an arrest record in Los Angeles and Atlanta."

"Do you think—could she have picked someone up?"

"It's possible," he said. "We're looking into that."

In which case, the person may not have called her, I thought. She would have had a web presence of some kind.

"Do you need to get into the deli now?" I asked.

"Tomorrow morning is okay, as long as you get there before anyone touches anything."

I told him I'd take care of it.

"Nash, was there a reason other than takeout that Tippi stopped by the deli?"

"She asked about the trumpet case," I said. "Told me it was special. I also think she wanted to connect to him somehow, visit the last place he'd been."

"I assume she didn't say anything about being concerned for her safety?"

"Not a word," I said. "She didn't seem anxious."

Sally called my name from the kitchen.

"Who's that?" Grant asked.

"I have guests."

"I thought you said you were napping?"

"I was," I said. "It's a little bit of a *magilleh*—can we talk about it some other time?"

"Sure," he said a little frostily. "Thanks for your help. I guess Anita Fong Chan will be there bright and early."

"I'll be there."

He hung up. So did I. I'm not sure who was faster on the draw.

I trudged back to the kitchen. The women had removed various items from their bags: candles, chalk, several big books, and some kind of deep finger bowl. I hoped it was not for blood. Or fingers.

"We should get started," Sally said.

"Of course," I replied. I looked at her. "You really heard someone say she was a teepee?"

"That's what it sounded like, though you can never be sure," Sally said. "The voices ride the wind and come into the smoke. The reception is not ideal."

"Do you ever—I mean—"

"Imagine things? Is it live or is it Memorex?" She laughed. "Everything is real, even if you imagine it. The question is, is it truth?"

That answer wasn't among the more helpful ones I'd ever received, but it was all I was going to get.

I led the way to the basement, which was down a flight of uncertain wooden steps to a hollow wooden door with a wobbly brass knob. The den beyond was a long, impersonal rectangle with cheap carpet and equally cheap wood paneling that was warping from the wall. It was furnished with secondhand everything, including flea market landscapes and mismatched lamps. I had added two of my childhood paint-by-number oils of little Dutch children that had been in a trunk. The whole point of the room was the pool table in the middle. My father was a big player.

"Nice," Sally said.

"You're kind."

Sally grinned. "Where *I* live? This is 'nice.'"

I felt like I'd been "served," a little. I didn't

come into contact with a lot of openly Native Americans back in Manhattan—which is kind of ironic, if you think about it.

"We're going to perform a consecration ceremony that combines the essence of Wiccan, Cherokee, Damballa, and Viking services," she said.

"Ah, multidenominational," I remarked nervously.

I had intended it as a joke. Apparently, it wasn't. Sally nodded gravely in accord as she scouted for a relatively worn-out spot in the carpet. Opening a door on the opposite side of the basement, she saw the boiler room, sniffed the metallic closeness of the place, tugged on the string light under a single bulb, then said that would be a perfect place. It was a small area with a concrete floor, bare cinder-block walls, an occasionally noisy old oil burner, and a cedar closet the previous owner had built. I used it to store unopened boxes of clothes and mementoes. Like most big-city dwellers, I'd lived a possession-light life in New York and hadn't accumulated much down here. I almost envied the Wiccans. They seemed to have few needs in order to produce what were to them big gains.

Leaving the single bulb on, Sally drew a chalk circle on the floor and a five-sided star inside of it. It was a pentangle, not a Star of David, though I wondered what kind of spirit *that* would invoke;

probably my *tante* Rose complaining about her girdle or my *feder* Sol looking for his false teeth.

The bowl was placed in the center of the star and the women gathered around the circle on their knees, a candle in front of each. I was not invited to join but stood to the side and was ignored. Which was fine with me; the room was scary enough with all its dark, secretive crannies that had never seen a flashlight. Now that the candles threw more writhing shadows into the mix, I was happy to be standing in the open doorway.

Mad held her book in one tiny open palm and read in a language that sounded Eastern European. Glancing over her shoulder, I saw that it was, in fact, English—backwards. I didn't try to read it. I'd had enough trouble with Hebrew for my bat mitzvah. I wasn't sure I wanted to know what it said.

After a few minutes of her reading and the other women occasionally repeating, the service passed to Dalila, who read a kind of clucking tongue from lines written in snaky undulations across her page. Sally continued in a language I didn't understand, looking at symbols that looked like petroglyphs, after which Ginnifer finished with a kind of grunting interpretation of runic symbols.

I had no idea how long the reading lasted; it could have been ten minutes, it could have been an hour. The candles must have had some kind of herbs or mushrooms baked into them because I felt woozy the entire time. I was leaning against the jamb, so I wasn't afraid I'd fall—*Like Lippy?* I thought with a passing jolt. It was more like I was safe in a dentist's chair with laughing gas. I didn't have visions, but reality seemed slightly distorted. It stopped within instants of the candles being snuffed out.

The women were standing. Their hands were pressed lightly together in front of them. Their eyes were shut, but their faces were turned to the bowl. Inside was one half of an apple lying skin down with the seeds plucked out. That was definitely unexpected—and weird. Unless Dalila had sneaked it in under her cloak, I didn't see any way they could have brought it down here. Or why. To fool me? I wasn't going to convert or anything. Sally had to know I didn't *really* care whether this was authentic, only that it was bona fide enough to pass the legal standard for "holy site."

The women were stationary for a few minutes, after which Sally broke away and the others followed. They appeared a little worn, unsteady.

"The she-spirit has blessed us," said Sally. "This ground is now sanctified."

"Just to make sure," I asked quietly, "that includes the den, right? Because that's where those guys wanted to dig."

"The area within the confines of the greater

structure is now sacred to the Earth Goddess," Sally droned, her eyes still shut—more like hooded, really, because the lids were vibrating a little. "The Great Goddess, through her servant, the serpent, first offered the apple to humankind in the Garden. She offered it anew today to refute the jealous God, He who sought to be the only God. Let Him be as He was at the beginning of things, the Patriarch God of Men. We are neither fearful nor moved by His violent, retributive ways."

I take back what I said; if that was the entirety of their faith, I could definitely sign on.

The women recovered their books. They left the bowl and apple.

"Leave that for now," Sally said.

"The bowl too?" I asked.

She nodded. "That'll keep mice from the Goddess's apple. We'll throw it out in the yard when Dr. Fassbinder has validated our service."

"Who?"

"The head of the theology department at the university," Sally said. She smiled. "Wiccan, Cherokee, African, and Jew—it's a minefield of political correctness no one will dare to challenge."

I felt as if my Aunt Rose's girdle had been loosened from my waist. "Thank you," I said. "Thank you very much."

"Thank *you*," she said. "The earth is no longer

unhappy. Now—you have any juice? Summoning the apple takes a lot out of us."

I did have some, though it wasn't really mine. I was all about vitamin water and diet soda, but healthy ole Grant, he liked to guzzle his morning juice. I hoped Sally would be pleased. In one of those ironies that threads through life, it happened to be apple.

Chapter 9

Anita Fong Chan came by shortly after we opened. She not only asked for my crullers and coffeepot, she asked if I ever use rat poison.

"Never," I said. "Just traps. And I've never had to empty one."

I didn't ask why. I knew. That's how Tippi had been killed. That told me something, as I'm sure it did Anita and Grant. The first murder, of Lippy, was planned. The second seemed improvised, and hastily. Then she asked a follow-up question that intrigued more than alarmed me.

"Do you use bamboo in any of your foods?"

I told her I did not. That was a puzzler.

I worked the kitchen. I didn't think I should be in the dining room, taking orders and interacting with human beings. I was tired, not having gotten to bed until after two, and then I was up at five. I was still a little woozy from whatever was in the candles, from the fact that I'd had a Wiccan ceremony in my basement, and from the reality, settling in, that Lippy and his devoted sister had both been murdered.

The phone rang in the kitchen. Thom was busy making change so I didn't expect her to grab the call. We don't do delivery and my vendors know to call on the office phone. So I assumed it was a wrong number or someone calling to ask for directions or else to arrange one of our rare catering gigs.

It wasn't any of those. It was Andrew A. Dickson III, attorney-at-law, legal advocate for *Dr.* Reynold Sterne, drummer-with-a-spoon of after-dinner mints, a man who made me wish we were Skyping because I wanted to see his face.

"I've called to arrange a time when the initial dig team can come and survey the interior property," he said all formal-as-you-please.

"Let me see," I replied. "Let me think," I added. And then I said, "They can't."

He sighed. "Ms. Katz, perhaps you need to revisit the terms of—"

"I don't need to revisit anything, Mr. Dickson the Third. My home is now a temple. No one is doing any excavating there."

"What are you talking about?"

"The structure has been blessed, bottom to top. Made hallow by a recognized priestess, witnessed by members of her congregation," I said. I read from the back of an envelope I'd stuffed in my bag the night before from while I was on the web. "By virtue of statute 501(c)(3), and subsets thereof, my Bonerwood abode is now recognized, by law, as being a site used for religious purposes."

The pause that followed was more than pregnant. It was bulging with quintuplets.

"What is the definition and affiliation of your church?" he asked.

"Wiccan," I said proudly. "It's a hive of the Nashville Coven."

"A hive?" he said flatly.

"That's right. It's how we witches describe a spin-off, a bud."

"*You* witches?" he said, less flatly. "You've been a Wiccan how long?"

"Since my priestess initiated me," I told him.

"What is the name of your priestess?" he asked.

"Sally Biglake."

"Of the Cherokee?"

"Of the Cherokee *Nation*," I corrected him.

Dickson was silent for a moment. "I recommend you get yourself an attorney," he said. "You will be needing one very soon."

"Thanks for the legal advice," I replied, and hung up.

* * *

It was a slow day—it happens, for no reason that I have ever been able to ascertain. Sometimes there are more tourists, less regulars. Sometimes the reverse. Sometimes both. Today was light on either and I decided to get out.

It wasn't quite so random as that. Ever since Tippi's visit, I'd been wanting to put some claws into Robert Barron. Some of that was my own unfinished business with his stupid, swaggering way and some of it was wondering if he had had a reason to swipe Lippy's trumpet case.

The Oak Slope Marina was a short drive east along I-40, located on the reservoir known as the J. Percy Priest Lake. There was a big sign at the entrance to the lake grounds themselves that talked about how the Percy Priest Lake was the home of the Stewarts Ferry Reservoir project, which was undertaken by the U.S. Army Corps of Engineers in 1946, renamed in 1958 to honor Congressman Priest, and was completed in 1967. The USACE still operated and supervised the dam, the power house, the lands and waters, and so on.

Once I reached the marina—self-described by a billboard that proclaimed A RESERVOIR OF FUN!—Barron's boat was easy to find. There was no cutesy nickname for his thirtysomething-foot SP Cruiser, which looked like a cross between a motorboat and a sailboat, gleaming white and proud in the sun. No, it was called simply and boastfully, *The Baron*. The gently rocking vessel was moored in a slip or a berth or whatever you call them, right where the land met the wharf or pier or whatever you call *them*. The entirety of my brush with boating was the Staten Island Ferry, and only then to take friends and relatives visiting Manhattan on a quick harbor scoot past the Statue of Liberty. I had never even taken a rowboat out in Central Park. When I crossed water, it was by bridges, tunnels, or air—and, once, in summer camp, on a rope.

I didn't know whether Barron would be there but chances were good: he'd had a bag of galley-type supplies when he was at the deli—toilet paper, veggies, and beer—so I hoped he intended to be here for a couple of days.

Maybe to get yourself a treasure map? I thought as I walked up the plank or ramp or whatever you call the boarding-thing toward the front of the boat.

There was a chain across the top. I stopped.

"Robert?" I called toward the back of the boat. "You here? It's Gwen Katz!"

I heard light footsteps.

Two sets of them.

Barron stuck his big head through a big window or porthole or whatever you call them. Another man stuck his head out the hatch or door, just beyond. I didn't know whether I had stumbled on a business meeting or a tête-à-tête. Possibly both.

Barron smiled crookedly. "Hi, Nash. Never expected to see you out here."

"Life is funny," I said vaguely.

"Come on aboard," he said. "Just unlatch the—"

"I see it," I told him. The hook-and-eye latch was about as complex as a half-century-old country fence. I saw one, once, when I was nine, visiting my great-uncle Oskar in Maine, where he'd retired because it reminded him of his native Croatia. Except for the lack of pogroms, or whatever they called the anti-Semitic attacks in the Balkans. A week after that visit, I had tetanus. I swore never to leave a city again. I hooked the chain back behind me as I boarded. "I'm not interrupting anything, am I?"

"Nothing that can't be continued some other time," Barron said. "Just planning an excursion."

"Sounds interesting," I said. And it might have been, too, if just being around Barron didn't make me seasick.

I walked in, past the other fellow. Barron was dressed in a blue jumpsuit that hugged his thickening-in-the-middle frame. The man with him was swarthy, about five-eleven, chiseled, with slightly Asiatic features. He was wearing a white t-shirt and swim trunks. He looked a little peaked. Barron introduced him as Yutu White.

"Gotta love those double entendre names, eh?" Barron roared, winking.

"They're a riot."

"He's an Inuvialuk, a Western Canadian Eskimo," Barron went on, either not having heard me or not caring what I had to say or both. "Not very happy to be on a boat, you may have noticed. Can you imagine? An Eskimo who has never been in a kayak."

White pointed to a brown bag on the table. I couldn't read the writing, but there was a picture of a wave on it. Dramamine, I guessed.

"Yeah, Robert, that's funny," I said. "Like a free-spending Jew."

He looked at me with an expression that suggested agreement. He didn't realize I was being ironic.

"Hi, Yutu," I said.

He nodded gently.

"Yutu says he knows the location of a Russian treasure ship from the early twentieth century," Barron went on.

"Shhh," White said.

"It's okay," I said. "I won't steal it."

"No, I meant he's talking too loud," Yutu said. "Use your inside-cabin voice, Robert, not your on-deck one."

"Nash isn't after my treasure. She's got plenty of her own." He winked again. God, what a boor. "It's a fascinating story about that ship," Barron said as he walked to a large chart table, which filled most of the room. Various maps were spread on it, held flat on the sides with empty beer bottles.

Barron pointed to one which bore Cyrillic labels and the date 1917. "It was reportedly full of Romanov treasure the Czar was trying to sneak out before he abdicated. Gold, jewelry, art, all kinds of things. A barge left Moscow and went north to Arkhangelsk where it was loaded onto a battleship of the Imperial Russian Navy. The ship skirted the Arctic, headed east, bound for Canada—where it was supposed to be met by agents of the dynasty. Never made it."

"Why?" I asked.

"Ice floes and storms, according to a letter we found from an officer with the Department of Fisheries and Oceans who was in the region where it was supposed to make landfall," Barron said. "Very severe weather that year."

"That would be quite a historic find," I said.

"It'd be colossal!" Barron said. "I"—he shot a look at Yutu—"*we* will be rich and famous!"

My eyes wandered around the table. The story was interesting, but not why I was here. I saw the top of a small map, with folds, that said Fiji—1790. Judging from what little I could see, it *might* have been just the right size to fold and tuck in a trumpet case. "What's this one?" I asked.

He looked where I was pointing, shuffled maps to cover it. "Nothing," he said. "South Pacific, dead end, not a happy story."

"Tell me," I said.

"Yes, I am interested, too," Yutu chimed in.

"Rather not," he said emphatically.

"Why?" I pressed. "You trusted me with your Russian warship—"

"This is different," he insisted. "Sorry . . . just a sore topic. Actually, Nash, Yutu and I should probably get back to work. He has to get back to the Great White tomorrow. If you want to visit after that . . . ?"

"Sure," I said. I was trying to think of some way I could bump or lean on the table top, knock everything over to get a better look at that other map. *Screw it*, I thought. I reached for where he had tucked it, found the corner, pulled it out. "Hey, there is just one thing I wanted to ask about this—"

Barron slammed a thick palm down on the map as the edge emerged. "Stop, dammit, you pushy J"—he caught himself and said more quietly—"jerk."

I smirked knowingly—there was nothing to add; he had shot his own fat foot—but I kept my eyes on the document to take in all there was to see. I saw a faded image on yellowing paper, a splotchy stain about an inch across, and a stamp of some kind, the first two letters of which were F–I.

Barron self-consciously neatened the pile, pushing the Fiji map back. He looked from me to Yutu. "I'll talk to you about this later," he said, and then his eyes snapped back to me. "I'm just under a lot of pressure right now. You probably should've called."

"Apparently," I agreed. "Sorry." I turned to Yutu. "Lovely meeting you."

"And you," he said with a polite bow.

I smiled thinly at Barron. "Next time you come in, breakfast's on me. That is, unless that's too 'pushy.'"

"No, it's very kind—you needn't have. I'm sorry. Thank you."

That was a fumble-mouth bunch of words befitting a ham-fisted grave robber and likely anti-Semite. I left, trying to ignore the low burn in my stomach. The fresh lake air helped a little. Thinking about that map helped a little more. Fiji isn't exactly around the corner from Hawaii, but it's in the same South Pacific part of the world. There were probably a lot of ways over many years that map of that region could have made its way to Oahu. From Oahu to Nashville, Tennessee? Not so many.

Most importantly, why was the big lug so anxious about it?

I thought about those tunas Barron was telling me about at the deli. How many would he have to catch and drain to get enough mercury to kill someone? Could you even do that to a tuna? Was it like draining the oil from a can of sardines? Or did you run it through a press, like one of those old-time laundry ringers. Was there something in the nautical world that required mercury, something that would justify Barron possessing it? That would be easy enough to find out.

Unfortunately, I didn't have time to do that research now. I had a text message from Luke:

THOM WAS JUST ARRESTED

Chapter 10

I Bluetoothed as I drove.

Luke answered the phone. "Murray's Deli."

"What happened?" I asked.

"That lawyer came in and Thom hit him," he said.

"You mean a slap? With her hand?"

"Side of the head with a bottle of Windex," he said. "The big full one for the front door."

"Aw, jeez. How are you guys holding up?"

"The girls are bussing their own tables—I'm on checkout," he said. "We called Dani to come in. I run back to do dishes when I can."

"Can you handle it?"

"If you don't care whether the bill drawer is a little screwed up—"

"I'll stop there first, help until Dani gets there, then bail Thom out," I said.

"They cuffed her," Luke said. "She was pretty

badass, though. She was still yelling over her shoulder as they hauled her out."

"Where's the lawyer?"

"Gone," Luke said. "I think he was afraid A.J. would come after him next."

I hung up, hit the gas, and got there before the rush descended. The place smelled of Windex. Whether she'd whacked him hard enough to pop the top or to split the plastic bottle, that would have been a nasty smack. I made a mental note to check my insurance. I think I was covered for violent outbursts by employees. My uncle had had some wild people in his employ before Nashville got civilized, infamous waitstaff like Belle deJeune, April "Red" Dragon, who was a Marxist, and—I kid you not—a busboy named R. Tillery. I was glad they'd moved on to greater callings, like a professional lawn mower, an expatriate living in Paris, and—I kid you not—a librarian.

It was busier than usual, word of Thom's exploits apparently having spread. The added crowd was mostly regulars who came to inquire as to her well-being and mental state. Most found it incredible that the serene, churchgoing Thomasina had snapped.

But not everyone: One was me; I saw how she had acted with Dickson during their first encounter. The other was Karen Kerr, who just happened to be getting out of jail while Thom was being ushered in.

Her six-foot, four-inch frame was hunched at the shoulders and her long blond hair hung carelessly around her lean-jawed face. She looked like Thor just back from a war with the Frost Giants.

We didn't know each other well enough to do more than exchange looks and tentative how-are-you? smiles. She glanced at a menu and just sat there, staring.

I took over the counter from Raylene, who just looked at me like a lamb who'd lost Bo Peep. Which she had. Thom was a shepherdess to us all.

"What can I get for you?" I asked K-Two.

"A job," she said.

"Sorry?" I asked.

"A Reuben with horseradish," she said in a deep voice, coated with a trace of what sounded like New England—Maine, maybe. "And a chocolate milk shake."

I wrote out the order, passed it to Newt. "Did you say you needed a job?" I asked.

She nodded glumly. "I need busywork. I don't want to think."

"Rough patch?" I asked, deciding to play dumb.

"Couple days in jail," she said. "They thought I killed that guy up the street. Then discovered I didn't. Then couldn't decide whether I contributed to it. Then decided I didn't. He blew his horn in my ear, startled me—like an air horn at a match, y'know?"

"I can imagine," I said, though I really *couldn't*

conceive of what it would be like to be in a cage with a roaring crowd, air horns, and someone trying to put you in a leg lock or worse.

"I came here because I heard at the pen that Thomasina took a swing at someone," she said. "She's so sweet. Guy must've really been a jerk."

"He *is* a jerk," I said.

The woman's blue eyes came up for the first time. "You know the dude?"

"I know him."

The woman's mouth twisted as she considered the information. Then her eyes went back down. "I'd go over to have a talk with him about not pressing charges, but—probably not a good idea right now."

"No," I agreed. "Not with the manslaughter thing you just got behind you."

"It's not just that," she said. "There's a commission that's part of the Mixed Martial Arts Federation. You get arrested, there's a waiting period—like buying a gun—when you're benched. I've got to wait for a formal hearing so I can present my case."

"Even though the charges were dropped?"

She nodded. "The murder charges, not the assault charges."

"But—the victim is deceased."

"Right, but a committee still has to review the police reports, my own statement, all of that stuff."

I slid over to take an order, then came back.

"That's a bum deal," I said, trying to pick up the lingo.

"Seriously. I was never even *in* a prison before," she said distractedly. "I mean, it's bad for the career, but it would have been a good place to stay in shape. Nothing to do except push-ups, crunches, jumping jacks, and sleep."

I moved to take another order, then returned.

"Speaking of what happened with Lippy, I am curious, though," I said. "You didn't happen to see anyone around you when he fell?"

She raised and lowered a shoulder. "Cops asked me that, too. Honestly? I was too surprised to pay attention. There was just this horn in my ear, a loud *blat* that made my elbow go sideways into his jaw, and he fell. Boom! I tried to grab him, but, I swear, it was like he was already on the way down when I turned. Which maybe he was, according to what I heard—that he was poisoned."

"Where'd you hear that?" I asked.

"From my lawyer," she said. "When I thought about it later, it made sense. It was like he was having a heart attack or something and just screamed into his horn." She shook her head as I handed her her meal. "Who would want to kill a musician? And his sister, too."

"I think Tippi was an afterthought," I told her. "I think someone killed Lippy to get his instrument case."

She looked up again with her mouth full of

corned beef, sauerkraut dangling from both sides. "What kind of sense does that make?"

"I don't know," I admitted. "I'm not a criminal."

I took an order for old Michael Dickles's matzo ball soup and dry rye toast on the other side of the counter.

"You really think that's *why* this happened?" she asked, washing her big bite down with milk shake. "The case? You don't think, maybe, someone pinched it for the money?"

"Why not just grab the cash, then?" I asked.

She thought for a second. "Because now that I think of it, there wasn't any," she said. "He was just starting the day."

"But don't these guys usually put a few bills in the bucket to encourage passersby to—," I said, but my voice trailed off. "Except that Lippy was broke," I said mostly to myself. "He didn't even have coins to drop in there." I wandered off to give Dickles his soup and toast, then drifted back.

"That means someone specifically wanted the case," K-Two said.

That spun my attention back to "Robber" Barron, but only for a moment. The crowd was growing and I was busy for the next half-hour until Dani arrived. Young, wide blue-eyed, eager-to-please Dani Petunia Spicer. Thom was a surrogate mother to the kid. She blew in through the door so firm of purpose that if it weren't for the nose piercing and spiky blond hair, I might not have recognized her.

She stripped off her coat like Diana Prince becoming Wonder Woman, locked eyes on me for a moment as she took my place, and said one word:

"Go."

I went.

I called Grant as I hurried to my car. He hadn't heard about Thom's arrest and—snapping into unemotional just-the-facts-ma'am policeman mode—he found out where they were keeping her, since I hadn't asked K-Two where she had been held.

Like a car that has been towed, I thought. *Just look it up, pass the info along, collect the bail.*

"She's at the Criminal Justice Center, 448 Second Avenue North," he said. "Bail hasn't been set—that'll come down in about an hour, after a judge has reviewed the charges against Ms. Jackson."

He was being cop-formal now, too. The woman who had always been "Thom" to him was now "Ms. Jackson." What a tin-eared dope. He always was "the job" before "the lover." I had just been too distracted by sex and companionship to see that.

"I wouldn't worry about it, though," he went on. "She's not a danger to the community, no likelihood of flight, not charged with a serious crime, nothing drug related. And the officers confiscated the evidence—a Windex bottle?"

"Yeah. I don't believe in generic."

He didn't get the joke. He never had.

"Anyway, I'm guessing it'll be five hundred bucks."

"Thanks," I said, hanging up as I punched the address into my GPS. I didn't feel like talking to him just then. Or maybe ever. Functional was the new boring.

I followed the calm, reassuring directions of the GPS voice, and pulled up to the six-story brick building that seemed darker and more dungeony than it probably was. I went to an imposing receptionist who sat behind bulletproof glass. She buzzed me into an area where an equally broad-shouldered lady clerk gave me a stack of papers to fill out. The pile of forms actually had weight that probably went to pounds rather than ounces. I was happy to see, announced right on the top of the first document, that I could charge Thom's bail.

After nearly fifty minutes of hand-cramping detail—how did people have all this information, like bank accounts and phone numbers for the last five years, at the ready in the criminal era before cell phones?—my credit card was taken and run through, after which I was instructed to wait. Everything said here was a short, monotone order. What were those Star Trek aliens? The one with the hive minds? That's who I felt I was with. I was informed that Thom was in a holding cell and would be brought to me. I stood—for a half-hour, it turned out—trying to think of what I would say to my poor, probably humiliated manager.

To my utter surprise, Thom not only came out proud, she was still angry. I could tell from the forehead-up tilt of her head and the tight line of her lips.

She was not handcuffed, but she was led by a big woman's firm grip on her forearm. I thought, distractedly, that I should ask for a job application and pass it along to K-Two. She'd fit in with the Amazons I'd seen here so far.

"I hear they have good locks here," I said.

It took a moment, but Thom got it and smiled. "Thanks for coming."

The hefty guard didn't leave until we were buzzed out and the door had clicked shut. "Thanks for coming to get me," Thom said as we stepped into the sunlight. She winced. I offered my sunglasses but she declined.

"What happened?" I asked.

"That attorney baited me," she said. "And I bit. He said he wanted to see you but I think he wanted to see me. I told him you weren't there and he started talking about my brother, about how they'd take your house the same way, by eminent domain, because the witch women hadn't registered their intent to open a temple—"

"That's not how eminent domain works," I said. I didn't know much about it, but I knew *that* much.

"I know, but I just snapped, Nash. I think he

rehearsed the whole thing. Didn't take a minute, about as long as he would've had to wait to see you if you were there."

We got in the car and drove back, me in thoughtful silence and Thom still venting. Over the course of the drive, she grew angrier at herself than at Dickson, alternately asking for the forgiveness of me and of Jesus, and—as she rambled—I think she actually became more and more enamored of the idea of being a martyr.

"That man is *bad*," was the mantra to which she kept returning, as if she were playing priest and parishioner both, and that was the congregation's response.

I knew that she would never get to be that martyr, of course, because the whole thing was a setup aimed at me. Sure enough, when we got back to the deli and Thom had taken up her post at the cash register—with happy smiles from the staff, which seemed to soften her mood considerably—I got around to checking my e-mails, and there was a message from His Academic Eminence to call him "at my earliest convenience, of course"—he was so proper and considerate now, I wanted to barf—to discuss "this morning's unfortunate but not irreversible situation."

The subtext, unwritten but unhidden, was: we'll drop the charges against Thom if you let us into your house. Thom would never have heard of it, naturally, but they had to know I would never let her arrest stand.

I called his cell right then, which was my earliest convenience, and he took the call.

"You both stink like bad salmon," I said in response to his "Hello, Ms. Katz."

"I'm glad to see you're not yet using 'witch' metaphors," he said. "When you do, I've smelled burning mandrake root and that's not so nice, either."

We both went silent. He was quick on the recovery, I'll give him that.

"Now that the pleasantries are out of the way," he went on, "why don't we look for a way out of this impasse."

"*A* way," I repeated. "Is there more than one?"

"There's always more than one choice," he said. "At minimum, there are two—a good one and a bad one."

"I hate you," I said.

"Understandable," he replied affably. "Nonetheless, how do you want this to go? And I mean realistically, not the 'good for me, bad for you' repartee of which you seem to be so fond."

I hated him even more right then. He wasn't just a bastard, he was a controlling man who had control over me like I was one of his damned students. It was tough to push that aside and think of Thom.

"You name the terms, I'll agree to them," I said.

"Wow," Sterne said. "That's frankly more than I hoped for—"

"With one provision," I added. "If your putz of an attorney shows up at the deli again, Thom is immune from prosecution for any harm that may befall him."

"Thom is a grown woman. She should be able to—"

"Hit the guy who did dirt to her brother, even if it was legal?" I said. "I agree. I want it in writing."

"What if he comes to your award-winning deli for lunch?"

Now the guy was just being difficult. "Then I might poison him myself," I said, hoping that Dickson didn't, in fact, subsequently go the way of Lippy and Tippi. I'd be in a pretty tough spot then.

"Ms. Katz, I don't know if we can indemnify Ms. Jackson against a murder—"

"Fine. Attorney Dickson does not come here, ever, for any reason," I said. "And I don't want him at my home, either. Those arc my terms."

"I'll talk to him—"

"Your word, now," I said. "I'll *futz* around with witches to protect my property, but you mess with my friends, we're at war. I will go down to my basement and take a pickax to the floor before you ever get near the place."

"Don't," he said. "Please. I agree. You'll never see Dickson again."

"Bring whatever you need me to sign to my house, tonight," I told him. "Eight o'clock. That includes a promise that Thom won't be prosecuted for what happened this morning."

"I don't know if I can make—"

"Come eight-o-one, I won't hear the door because of all the chopping."

"I'll be there," he promised.

I hung up feeling good for having stood up to the guy, but bad for what I had just committed to let them do. I decided to leave the rest of my e-mails till later and figured, as far as the dig was concerned, that was that and I'd just have to live with it.

But in the life of any human being, when is "that" ever really "that"?

Chapter 11

I worked in the dining area the rest of the day and left after making sure that Thom wasn't going to suffer a delayed reaction to the traumatic events of the morning.

"I'll be okay," she assured me. "Me and Lord Jesus have a good working relationship. I pray to Him and He supports me when I'm uncertain. In fact, I spoke to Christ in jail—along with my cellmate, Françoise Shabazz."

I commented on the unusual combination of those names and Thom said she was a French African woman being held for a visa violation. It made sense, but it still sounded strange.

Since Jesus seemed to have things well under control, and the camaraderie of the staff seemed to buoy Thom, I felt all right when they left—Dani and Luke, who were an item, taking her to a new

frozen yogurt shop for a shake or two. I quietly
prayed that Dickson didn't have a similar craving.

I made a pastrami on rye with mustard to go,
got home around seven-thirty, fed the cats, and
was just sitting down to eat when my "that was that"
got flipped on its ear.

It wasn't Robert Barron or Grant Daniels or even
Andrew Dickson who showed up at my door—
adversarial people and one annoyingly neutral
person who had actually played a part in my day.
No, with the growl of a motorcycle and the slam-
ming of car doors, it was my friends. My *new*
friends. Or, rather—as they called themselves—my
sisters.

It turns out that in the Wiccan world, establish-
ing a temple means just that: you've set up a house
of worship where people could come and pray. For
Wiccans, that turned out to be at night when there
was a moon and stars, owls hooting on chimneys,
and a general quieting of mechanized society.

At least, that's how Sally Biglake explained it
when she showed up at my door with Mad and a
small group of women I did not know.

"I didn't realize that consecration means my
door is always open," I said.

Sally seemed genuinely surprised. "What *did* you
think it meant?"

I couldn't tell her the truth; I thought it meant
absolutely nothing.

"May we come in?" Sally pressed.

I stepped aside, not without some reluctance, and the women filed in. There were six in addition to Sally and Mad. My cats fled their dinner bowls when they entered—something they never did with strangers.

"How often will you be having these gatherings?" I asked.

"Every new moon, every night of the full moon, and every Samhain," she said. Before I could ask, she said, "That is the end-of-summer celebration marking the final harvest and the arrival of dark winter. Typically, on November first."

"Great," I said. "You can help eat my trick-or-treat candy."

"That's very considerate," Sally replied.

This was going to be terrible. The woman had no sense of irony. She wouldn't see that this whole thing was a really bad joke.

"Don't you have other temples you can use to kind of spread the worship?" I asked.

"It is customary to use the site that has been most newly sanctified," she replied.

"Well, here's the thing," I said. "In about fifteen minutes, a man is coming who, through a strange series of circumstances, I've had to agree to let dig in the—the *temple*. You should probably bless some other place because this one isn't going to be available for a year or so."

The look that settled on her wide face could best be described as war-painted minus the paint.

It was little Mad who stepped forward and said, "Do you realize what you've done?"

"I think so," I said. "I've obviously inconvenienced all of my, uh—sisters."

"You've done far, far worse," Mad said, pointing at me with a crooked finger. "You have made us unhappy."

"I'm truly sorry," I said. "It was either that or watch my friend, someone who is very dear to me—like a sister, a true sister—go to prison."

"We are not your sisters?" Mad asked with a wounded expression.

"Apparently, we are not," Sally declared.

"No, it isn't like that," I insisted. "We *are* a little sorority. But I thought the purpose here was to prevent an unhappy earth, right? To keep the bad guys from digging up the camp of the dead."

Sally came closer. I smelled ugly weed on her clothes. I wondered if it was burned mandrake root.

"You used us," she said.

"That's not true," I replied.

The other women were moving around in a kind of semicircle. I was starting to get a little scared. Whoever would have thought that my cats were smarter than me? Besides them, I mean.

I was considering making a dash for the bedroom and barricading myself inside when the doorbell rang. It was like a church bell on All Hallows dawn, when all the frolicking demons go home. The women stopped and looked to Sally. I took that opportunity to shoot over to the front door.

"Dr. Sterne," I said, ridiculously loud and welcoming. "Come in!"

He seemed as surprised as I was by the effusive greeting. I almost slammed the screen door in my eagerness to admit the big man onto my campus. He entered and hesitated, obviously confused by the gathering. He was clutching his worn leather portfolio tightly, as if it were a life preserver.

"We sisters were just having a little impromptu meeting of the hive of the Nashville Wiccan Coven," I explained.

"We did have an appointment—?" Sterne asked.

"Absolutely," I assured him. "And appointment trumps impromptu," I said to Sally.

If looks could kill—and perhaps they *could,* with this band of necromancers—I was not long for this world. Sally looked from me to Sterne to the ceiling. She turned her hands palm up and held them before her bosom, as though they were supporting an invisible cup.

"The tears of the One Source, the Divine Incarnate, flow on this, our sacerdotal womb," she said. Her eyes drifted down to me. "We shall all know sadness until the earth is once again joyful." The others raised their hands like hers and they all shut their eyes. And in a mournful voice accompanied by her own tears, Sally intoned with the others:

> *Mar to ainghlich is naoimhich*
> *A toighe air neamh.*
> *Gach duar agus soillse,*
> *Gach la agus oidhche,*
> *Gach uair ann an caoimhe,*
> *Thoir duinn do ghne.*

When they were finished, they began to hum.

Sterne leaned toward me. "That was Celtic," he whispered. "A prayer, I think."

"Saying what?"

"The only words I recognize are *ainghlich is naoimhich*, 'angels and saints,'" he said. "I would imagine they are asking for celestial help."

"Swell."

The humming stopped a few seconds later and, as one, the women opened their eyes. From somewhere in the distance—the bathroom off my bedroom, it sounded like—the cats mewed miserably in unison. Smiling, Sally left, the women falling in behind her.

I watched them vanish in the darkness, then turned to Sterne. "Well, that was New Age-y," I said.

"Old Age-y is a more apt description," he said. "Fourth or fifth century B.C., I would guess."

He had corrected me in that professorial manner that reminded me of just one more reason why I didn't like him. We stood in dumb silence for a few moments after that. I realized I had nothing to say to this self-serving jerk who had helped set up dear Thomasina for a fall.

"You have papers for me?" I asked, turning my back and walking to the sofa. I slid behind the coffee table and sat.

He unzipped the pouch and stood there. "It doesn't have to be like this."

"Yeah, it does. Extortion is a dirty business."

"I'm truly sorry about that," he said. "Bringing in a coven wasn't exactly fair play, either. And from where I stood, those Wiccans seemed none too pleased."

"I was desperate," I said.

"So was I," Sterne replied. "This research we're doing is important. Your uncle lived here long enough to understand that. We're trying to retrieve history that has been plowed over. He said something to the effect that, as a kid, he was always frustrated by the fact that there were no pictures of Moses or Abraham or Solomon."

I had been staring at a dent in the carpet made by the leg of the sofa. I looked up at him. "Uncle Murray said that?"

"On the record at a town council meeting," Sterne said. "There are descendants of the African Americans who lived here who feel the same—"

There was a sharp rap against the front window that caused us both to start. I stepped over, saw a small crack in the glass, and went outside. A dead bat was lying belly up on top of the rose bushes in front of the window. Its head was bloodied. I looked across the yard. At the edge of the yellow glow cast by the porch light, I saw the Wiccans standing by the street, pointing at me.

It was too far for them to have actually thrown the poor—but disgusting—little creature. It must have flown right into the glass.

"Please go or we'll call the police," said my knight in shining tweed.

"Call whomever you wish," Sally said. "*You* are the trespassers, not us. We will be back to see that our pact is not perverted."

"Hey, I have a bat, too," I said. "His name is Louisville."

The women stepped back into the darkness. I heard engines start, saw headlights snap on, and in a minute they were only distant sounds on the rural street.

"You have gardening gloves and a Baggie?" Sterne asked, looking over at the dead bat.

"I've got a shovel," I said. "I'll deal with it—but thanks."

We went back inside to finish our business. Sterne withdrew a manila folder and sat beside me. There was the letter I had requested along with three copies of my uncle's signed agreement with the university—to which a new line had been added for my signature. I signed without reading it.

He left one copy of the agreement and the letter promising to drop the charges against Thom.

"Is there any way I can make this better?" he asked as he put the letters back in the pouch. The zipping noise made me wince. It sounded final, impersonal, but triumphant—which it was.

"Not that I can think of," I said. "But there is one thing you can do for me."

"What's that?"

"You're going to hire some kind of security, right?"

"Yes," he said. "The campus uses—"

"I want you to hire a woman I know," I said.

"Has she been bonded?"

"I haven't a clue," I told him. "But she's a good woman who needs a job."

"You understand, Ms. Katz, that's not typically the kind of recommendation we seek—"

"You asked me a question, I answered," I said. "Her name is Karen Kerr and she's a mixed martial arts fighter."

"K Two?" he said.

"Yes," I replied. "How do you know her?"

"She gives self-defense instruction at the school," he said. "My kid sister has taken her classes."

"Good," I said. "She's out of work right now and I think she'd be willing to start tomorrow."

"Ms. Katz, this usually takes a little time," he

said. "There's paperwork to process and we won't even be on-site for another—"

"Tomorrow," I said. "Or didn't you notice—your Civil War campground is under assault from Wiccans and kamikaze wildlife."

He thought for a moment, then took out his cell phone and started texting. "You have a very good point," he agreed. "I'm letting my site director know."

I sat back and looked at the window. "How the hell did they do that?" I muttered.

"Probably a dog whistle," he said. "Something to interfere with the bat's echolocation."

"Or, it could be witchcraft," I said, mostly to myself.

Sterne snickered. "Please. You didn't do this because you subscribe to their belief in the supernatural." He glanced at me as he poked at his phone. "Did you?"

I noticed my sandwich, took a bite, went back to staring at the carpet. I had never believed in ghosts—not even as a little girl, when my grandma told me she had once met a dybbuk, the wandering soul of the dead.

"It was in a hayloft in Rovinj, Croatia," she had said when she was baby-sitting. *"I was resting from milking the cows and I heard it stirring. It spoke in a terrible voice and I ran away. It was gone when I returned with my father."*

I was ten and I half believed her for about two

years, until my great-uncle Oskar confided, at her funeral, as we were walking from the gravesite, that it was him and her best friend Milanka who were up in that hayloft.

"Your Grandma Vesna wanted ghosts and angels to be real because it meant there was a world after this one," he told me. *"So to her, they were real. But you must not confuse wishes with truth. Do not accept the ridiculous when there is a logical explanation."*

I told him, honestly, that the spirits of the dead were easier to imagine than him making out with a great-aunt Milanka.

He'd smiled a big smile and laughed when I'd said that. The other funeral-goers had looked at us with open horror, but it was our best moment together. On those rare occasions when my cranky uncle laughed, the wrinkles and the dentures and the tired, watery eyes seemed to vanish into an aura of renewed youth.

"You are right, Gwenka," he'd said, using his term of endearment. *"A ghost does make better sense."*

"Ms. Katz?"

I heard my name and looked at Sterne. "Yes?" I had forgotten—was there a pending question?

"What *do* you believe?" he asked.

"I believe that my carpet needs to be cleaned," I told him.

"What does that have to do with the spirit world?"

"Nothing, unless the guy who used to do my mother's Persian rugs is listening." I had another bite of sandwich, then wrapped it back up. "Time for you to go," I said.

Sterne seemed a little surprised. He stood with his portfolio tucked neatly under his arm. "So—no peace pipe?" he asked.

"I'm not kicking you out," I said. "That's something."

"All right, then," he said with a formal little bow, "if that's how you want it. I'll be in touch."

"When?"

"Tomorrow," he said as he turned to go.

"Dr. Sterne?" I said.

He turned warily. With good reason. "Yes?"

I walked over to him, watching the curiosity play out in his lips, which moved expectantly, like little caterpillars. They didn't know whether to smile, talk, or purse.

"You want to know what I believe?" I asked. "That I have a conscience. I feel bad about misleading those women, I truly do. But you? I don't believe you feel that you did anything wrong."

The caterpillars straightened. "You're right," he agreed. "I don't."

Sterne left on the other side of a big bang from the screen door. I felt very alone then, not because he was gone, but because everyone was. This reminded me of how much I missed everyone I'd ever known well or cared about—and everyone who knew about me.

"Gramma, *are* you here?" I asked hopefully

when Sterne had driven away. "Anybody? Uncle Oskar? Uncle Murray?"

Silence.

I put the rest of my sandwich in the refrigerator and noticed that the cats were back eating their dinner—the cowards. I looked around at the emptiness, I looked *in* at the emptiness, and I thought enviously of Thom, out with the staff. Why didn't I join them?

Because you are not, and never have been, a social party girl, I reminded myself. Not in high school, not in college, not on Wall Street. *You did your job, you went home to your husband, you had lunch with your mother or a few girlfriends, and that was life.*

You came here to change that, I pointed out to myself. Partly to get away from the past, but also to change.

Which did not mean fraternizing with the people I saw all day or men I didn't really want to see at all. Which left just one thing to do. Three, actually. First, I went to check the window the bat had hit. Quite a *zetz*. Actually shattered the double pane. Next, I got a food-prep glove, slipped it on, went outside, and picked up the bat. He felt like a toy, fuzzy and warm—albeit one that had been dropped in ketchup. I put him in a Baggie and placed the thing in my handbag. When that was done, I slipped on a leather jacket—a freebie from one of my meat suppliers, not a holdover from my rebellious streak, which had lasted about a semester in college when I'd taken Salina Buben's course in matriarchal socialism—then grabbed my keys and went out to do what I apparently did best.

Make trouble.

For myself.

Chapter 12

The silhouette of Robert Barron's boat hulked in the dark. There were no onboard lights, which meant he was either sleeping or out.

Sleeping at nine p.m. on one of the few days he was in town? Not likely. Out with his Eskimo pal? Much more likely.

I decided to go aboard. The good thing about being a woman is I could always say I was there to see him and, not finding him there, I waited. He would probably be too surprised and maybe a little too tipsy to question that. If Yutu White was with him, I could sow jealous confusion and slip away.

I didn't know if any of that was practical. But it kept my mind off the fact that I had signed over the rights to my den. That made me want to cry.

The pier sounded creakier at night. I took out my cell phone and pretended to talk on it, like I wasn't afraid to be seen or heard. I waved into the dark, in case someone saw me, acting as if I belonged there. There were sounds from inside and outside the boat next to Robert's, but no one paid me much attention. I climbed the plank-thing onto the deck, passed my nemesis the skinny, sagging chain, went to the main cabin, and tried the door. It was locked, of course. So were the windows.

Enter the culprit.

I took the bat-Baggie from my purse and emptied the tiny corpse onto the deck. It slid clingingly from the plastic and hit the floor with a soft little thud. Then, stepping just above him, I drove my right elbow hard into the window.

That did nothing but hurt my elbow. Chastened, the next time I hit the window I used my keys wrapped inside a kerchief. The window didn't just crack, it shattered. It sounded like a breaking beer bottle, which was probably a good thing. The shards fell on the dead bat, which was perfect. He was buried in the fruits of his "crime," even though he looked so tiny there, I wasn't sure anyone would buy it. Unfortunately, I didn't think I'd be able to find a dead seagull before I left. This would have to be the story.

I zipped my leather jacket so I wouldn't cut myself on the fragments that still jutted from the window frame, then—looking around to make sure no one had heard, or cared much if they did—I crawled in like a Washington Square Park squirrel going along a branch: in spastic little fits. There was an armchair under the window, so at least I had the back of it on which to support myself, push-up style, as I maneuvered my hands onto the armrests and drew my legs in after me. It was inelegant and I grunted a lot, but I made it.

A light came on as I got my feet under me.

"You could have just knocked," a voice said from across the room.

I stood there, stupidly looking at Yutu White. I say stupidly because I was not only busted, I was overdressed for the occasion. He was on the sofa, propped on an elbow, his other hand on the base of a lamp. He was shirtless and pantless, save for some brief briefs, under a thin top sheet. He was wincing from the brightness and shielded his eyes.

"I thought it was just Barron drinking on the pier," he said. "But that is clearly not the case."

"No," I said.

"You want to flip off the Cruisair beside you?"

"The what?"

"The air conditioner—I don't appear to need it anymore."

I looked around, saw the grill in the wall. There was a knob beneath it. I put my bag on the floor and turned it. "Quiet little thing," I said admiringly.

"Yes. I like the cold."

"I guess you would have to," I replied.

"Right. Because I'm an Eskimo."

"I guess that was a little stereotyped," I told him. "I'm, uh—I'm Gwen Katz. In case you forgot."

"I had not," the man replied, sitting up. The action seemed to discomfit him slightly.

"Are you okay?" I asked.

"Yeah. Just some lingering seasickness."

"Are you taking anything for that?"

He grinned. "You mean like pills or—chicken soup, isn't it?"

I smiled. It really was annoying when the shoe was on *my* foot.

"Barron is not here," Yutu said. "I have to be awake very early so I turned in."

"Right. You said you were leaving tomorrow. Sorry to disturb you."

He blinked out sleep. "Now that you have, why are you here? I assume not to see Barron, or you would have telephoned."

"No," I admitted. "I'm looking for a trumpet case."

I knew how utterly ridiculous that sounded. So did Yutu.

"Yours?" he inquired.

"No. It belonged to a dead man."

That sounded even sillier. Yutu dug the heels of his palms into his eyes. "There was a proverb of which my father was most fond," the man said. "*If you are going to walk on thin ice, you might as well dance.*" He looked at me. "You are surely dancing."

"I am," I agreed.

"Don't be bashful," he said. "I do it, too."

"I don't usually—well, maybe I do—but there's a reason," I went on. "A trumpet player was killed the other day—"

"A friend?"

"No, just—" I hesitated. Yutu was sitting on the sofa in just his briefs. He had smooth, heavily muscled legs. Probably from all that ice dancing. "Do you want to put on a robe or something?"

"Actually, the night air feels good," he said. "Let's get a little cross-ventilation going." He reached behind him and cracked the window. "So this person you know was killed—"

"A man named Lippy, a street musician," I said, focusing on the lamp but seeing his not-quite-six-pack, but close enough, abs. "He was sitting next to Barron in my deli where he was apparently poisoned. After he left and was about to play down the block he collapsed and died. As he lay there, his trumpet case was pinched."

"And you suspect Robert?"

"I don't suspect him," I said. "I'm just curious. There's reason to believe—a slight reason, I'll grant you—that there was a map hidden inside."

"You believe this because . . . ?"

"Lippy bought the trumpet at a hock shop in Hawaii."

"A hock—?"

"Pawn shop," I interrupted. "One that specializes in sailing memorabilia."

"That's pretty thin."

"Like the ice," I agreed. "But that's not all. The next day, I met Lippy's sister when she came up to Nashville. She was murdered too. Before she died she said her brother had been e-mailing her about a treasure, but he never told her what it was."

Yutu nodded then lay back on the sofa. I half turned, saw the chart table, went over. I began sifting through the papers looking for something that could be folded and stuck in a case. Barron had straightened up since I'd been here; the Fiji map was gone. *Normal housekeeping or . . . ?*

"You're not a police officer, are you?" Yutu asked.

"No. But I dated one. Briefly."

"Then what is your interest in this matter? I ask because, as an impartial outsider, I might mistakenly suspect that you are after this hypothetical map for your own greedy purposes."

"Hey, I used to work on Wall Street," I said. "There are easier ways of making money than treasure hunting."

He laughed.

"No," I said. "I'm just—curious."

"No one breaks into another man's igloo because he is 'just curious,'" he said. "Either he is cold or hungry or seeking company."

I reflected on that. "I'm bored," I said. "Empty and disappointed and restless enough to take stupid chances. Oh, and angry."

"At whom?"

I said, "Myself. Why are *you* here? Did you know Barron before this?"

"No," he said. He got back up on an elbow. Now he looked like a *Playgirl* centerfold. "I wanted to do something for my mother and father. He still takes his fishing boat out every morning but it's hard work, and cold, and dangerous, and he should be retired." Yutu laughed. "How I wish I were on that boat now, in rough seas, instead of here."

"Am I that unwelcome?" I asked. Okay, I was fishing . . . I knew he didn't mean me. But I needed to hear something positive.

"You?" he said. "No, you're—"

Don't say "a challenge" or "funny" or—

"—terrific."

Okay, I thought. *That would do.*

"And attractive," he added.

Even better.

"Stop, I'm blushing," I said ham-fistedly. "I only look good compared to 'Robber' Barron."

"Please, you're not even from the same species," he said.

"Are you not having fun with him?" I asked as I finished fingering through the thinned-out pile.

"He's a necessary evil," Yutu said. "Most daredevils are slightly unhinged. They have to be."

"Have you known many adventurers?" I asked. I began wandering around the cabin, looking for trumpet-case-size hiding places, hollow sections in the bookcases behind tomes of seafaring and various other atlases.

"I've known a few," he replied. "Mostly the usual breed—mountain climbers, dog-team racers, skiers. There have been a few oddballs, like scientists who think it's a good idea to go seventy-five thousand feet up in a balloon to study solar storms. Also, before you decide to break anything else, I don't think he would have kept the trumpet case if he'd stolen it—why would he? There's a big lake out there he could have thrown it in."

"Did he take the boat out while you were here?"

Yutu shook his head. "But he could have dropped it anywhere along the shore. Or filled it full of rocks and dropped it. I'm usually a sound sleeper. Also, there's something else you should consider."

"What's that?"

"That Barron may be innocent," Yutu said. "Of this crime, anyway."

"Is that what you think?"

"I have absolutely no idea," he said. "But you can't rule it out, can you?"

"No," I admitted.

"Sometimes, scoundrels are just that and no more. I knew of a man who liked to eat dolphin meat, which was legal—though the killing of dolphins was not. When a dolphin was found dead and gutted, he was blamed. Until the polar bear that actually did the killing showed up." Yutu lay back down again. "I have to sleep—I have a long trip ahead of me. Do you think you can nose around some other time?"

"How about if I check in the back room? I'll shut the door."

"I'll still hear you," he said.

"Well, this *is* supposed to be a break-in, even if I tried to use a dead bat to cover it up," I pointed out.

"Despite which, I did not call the police," he said.

"Yes, why didn't you?" I asked. "Could it be that you aren't especially fond of Barron?"

"I'm not," he laughed, "but the truth is that your ploy was so incredibly inept I felt sorry for you."

I didn't like that explanation very much. "I don't need your pity, Yutu."

"That's true," he replied. "But you *could* use my help."

"How?"

"Barron usually comes back in a very happy mood, quite talkative," Yutu explained. "If he knows anything about the trumpet case, that would be the time to ask him."

"Makes sense. What time would that be?"

"Probably around midnight. That's when the Seashore Hoist closes."

"Right. I know the place."

He shrugged. "So, you can wait here with me, I'll verify the bat story, he'll draw the reasonable conclusion about *why* you're here, and you can chat him up before getting away clean."

"The reasonable conclusion being that I slept with you."

"Exactly," Yutu said. "He'll never believe that I actually *did* sleep for those two or three hours. You can hang out on the deck if you want."

I liked that even less. Was I completely resistible? Had I reached a place where the offense was in the *absence* of an advance? For the first time in a long time I was actually rooted where I stood.

"Or you can stay with me," Yutu said. "That would be more convincing."

And now I was completely *famisched* thanks to a smorgasbord of options. I told myself to relax. I didn't realize how tense I was until my shoulders went down.

"Let's be convincing," I said and walked over. I didn't know what to do next, though. Sit, lie, take off just my shoes—I wasn't sure what he really meant.

Thank God he held out his hand to me. It was a lifeline drawing me in. I still didn't know what I really wanted, but I wanted to be wanted and went with it. Yutu made all the decisions after that. Whatever nausea he may have felt when he was vertical did not impact him horizontally.

It was a wonderful and unexpected turn in the road. Until Barron's early arrival with a drinking buddy.

One I was not pleased to see.

Chapter 13

"What the *hell* happened to my boat?"

I woke to the voice of Robert Barron bellowing through the opening I'd made. I thought I recognized the voice of the person who was with him; I was still drowsy and couldn't be sure.

I hadn't intended to fall asleep. The truth is, until I got under the top sheet, I wasn't sure what I intended to do. That didn't happen until Yutu pulled the rest of my arm across his very smooth, very hard midriff. So I did that, and then more, and then I closed my eyes, and the next thing I knew—after a dream about Great-uncle Oskar milking cows—I heard Barron's voice and the chirrup of a woman.

"Jesus, no," I muttered as I placed the voice.

I didn't jump from Yutu's arms—which were still around me, and he was still asleep. I was on my side, my bare back to the door. I lay there waiting to see what happened.

"Damn, damn, and damn," Barron said. "Do you see this, Candy?"

"It's a bat," she said. "Poor thing must have been chasing mosquitoes or small winnow mayflies and *whammo.*"

"*That* little fur ball broke ten-millimeter-thick panes?"

"It may not have been just the bat," Candy said. "The window and the hull expand at different rates. That puts stress on the sealant. I'll bet the glass was kind of wobbly when the little guy hit and it just snapped."

"Did you do a report on boat windows?"

"I've done a report on everything," Candy said. "Twice. That's why I want to know more about this trip of yours. But this—Hec, get a shot of this."

"Yo."

I felt a burning in my belly. A bad one. A bright white light flashed on and I saw jagged, translucent marks on the wall I was staring at with wide, horrified eyes. My own shape was there as well, right past the still-sleeping Eskimo.

"Well, there's a how-de-do," Barron snorted.

"What?" Candy asked.

I saw the shadow of a pointing finger. "Yutu, you tawny little rascal," he said to no one in particular.

A head joined the finger on the wall. "Oh, this is wrong," Candy said.

Thank you, God, I thought—prematurely, as Yutu woke then and turned toward the window. He covered his eyes against the light.

"Robert?"

"Yeah, sorry—"

"No, it's okay," Yutu said. "We were waiting for you and fell asleep—would you kill the flashlight?"

"We?" Barron asked.

"Yeah, Gwen—" he rocked me gently with his butt. "Robert's back."

That didn't prove there wasn't a God. Just that I was not on his list of favorites.

Or maybe it's the witches, I thought. *They've cursed me.*

"Gwen . . . *Katz*?" Candy said with the kind of hungry enthusiasm reserved for celebrities or heads of state.

"Hi, all," I said over my shoulder.

"Who else is out there?" Yutu asked, obviously confused.

"Candy Sommerton, WSMV-TV News," she said.

"And Hec Paladin, camera operator," said the other man.

"We were shooting an act at the bar when Mr. Barron told us about his next venture," she said. "We thought it would make a terrific story."

"Wow, that's a long day for you, isn't it?" I asked.

"I'm filling in for Donna Meeche on the morning show this week," she said. "Say, do you want to put on clothes? That sheet doesn't hold much back."

"Or much backside," Barron added with a chuckle.

"Right," I said, still watching the whole thing play out on the wall. "Maybe if you killed the light, like Yutu asked?"

"Sure, sure," Candy said. "And then maybe we can do that interview we discussed? If now isn't convenient, perhaps tomorrow?"

The light remained on. Apparently, my submission was the price of throwing the off switch.

I hesitated as my mother and I argued in my head. I won. "Actually, tomorrow isn't good for me, either," I said as I threw off the top sheet, stood, gathered my clothes from the floor, and quickly dressed in the darkness of the vessel. When I was finished, I headed for the nearest door, which of course was the bathroom. Or, I think they call it a "head" but that sounds pretentious, so I refuse to. Undaunted, I turned around and went out the main hatchway. Candy and Hec were still standing there with Barron. The light had been snapped off. Through the broken window, I saw Yutu looking for his briefs.

"On the photo of Barron and Nancy Pelosi," I called in to him.

"Thanks."

"Do you know Nancy Pelosi?" Candy asked Barron.

"We—went sailing, once," he said evasively.

I looked at the odd little grouping. They were quietly discussing the local bat population and Barron's experiences with them around the world. Though they were facing in my direction, collected around the bat, none of them looked at me when I came over.

"During the nineteenth century, guano deposits were actually mined on Baker Island in the Central Pacific, used in fertilizer and explosives," Barron was saying.

"Now there's a ship I wouldn't have wanted to be on," I remarked. "Crap piled high—what a stench. Hey, wait. It has something in common with this boat. Let me think what that could be."

"Now hold on, Gwen," Barron said. "Don't diss *me*. All *I* did was come home to my own boat—"

"Where you gawked at my ass and made jokes and failed to safeguard the honor of a guest of *your* guest—which, if I'm not mistaken, is something no Eskimo would ever do. Am I correct in that, Yutu?"

"That is true," he agreed from the other side of the broken glass. "An Eskimo would not. Nor a gentleman."

Barron fired him a disapproving look, but Yutu didn't flinch. Even if it only lasted the night, at least the guy showed some loyalty to his lovers. His host backed down, looked at me. "Okay, sorry," Barron grumbled. "That was—not very chivalrous of me."

"Apology accepted," I said. I turned toward Candy and Hec. It was her turn to retreat.

She got the message. "Robert, we can do your mission profile some other time," she said. "We should really get to work on the video. Of that band."

"Right. Sure." Barron went back to looking at his broken window—he was still evidently puzzled by the impact of the bat—then shrugged and went inside. Hec went down the plank, the newswoman putting the chain back and shooting me a hostile look followed after him, vanishing into the darkness.

I wasn't certain how I'd gone from a person who simply wanted privacy to being an enemy, but somehow that transition had been made. Which was fine. I couldn't imagine anyone except a narcissist or an undemanding male actually wanting to be around Candy.

Which brought me back to my host.

I followed Barron in, mouthing a *thank you* at Yutu. He winked and went into the bathroom—how could I have mistaken it for an exit?—leaving us alone. Barron had been drinking, but not much. Or else he could hold his liquor really, really well. He sat heavily on the edge of his chart table.

"So, yeah, I guess that was pretty rude of me," Barron went on. I didn't stop him. The more he flagellated himself, the more he might talk to me.

"I just didn't expect anyone to be here. Least of all you."

"I surprise myself sometimes," I admitted. "I've been distracted—just trying to forget."

"Forget what?" he asked, taking the bait like a big carp.

"Lippy Montgomery," I said, shaking my head. "What happened to him really hit me hard."

"It did? I mean—did you know him well?"

"Only as a customer," I said. "But he seemed unusually distracted that morning."

"He did?"

I gave Barron a chance to think back. "Didn't he?" I asked.

"I don't think so," Barron said. "He was whistling the whole time. Pretty annoying. I tried to ignore him, mostly."

That's right, I thought. Lippy was—I wouldn't say he was exactly whistling, but "hissling."

"I got the feeling," I said, "from the way he was hugging that case of his, that it was something really precious. Maybe that's what made him anxious."

Barron snorted. "He spilled a little juice on it, is probably why. Wiped it off with his sleeve. That could be it."

"That wouldn't explain why he was hugging it," I mused.

"Maybe it just looked that way to you," Barron said. "I didn't notice that he was. Anyway, you said you were trying to forget him. So why are you talking about him?"

"It's how I forget," I said.

He looked at me as if I were a talking squid. "You're strange," he decided. "So, what's happening? Are you staying with Yutu? I can make myself scarce—"

"No, he needs to rest," I said.

Barron smirked.

"Because he's getting up early," I said. What was it with men and sexual innuendo? Did they have no other default setting? "But there is something I wanted to tell you, now that you're here."

"Oh?"

"Yes, that Fiji map?" I said. "Sorry I upset you before."

He stiffened. "It's all right," he said.

Our eyes locked for the briefest moment, and I confess, I considered it: we were standing about four feet apart and I thought about moving closer, trying to coax him out with irresistible Katz pheromones. But I balked. I had already caved to one *schmuck*, Reynold Sterne. That was my quota of self-abuse for the week.

"I've never been there," I said. "What's it like?"

"I was there for two weeks," he said. "It was overcast every day."

"What were you there for?"

"Look," he said, "I really don't want to talk about Fiji or the map. In fact, I'm kind of tired, so if you are leaving—I've got to put something over that window and then I'm going to turn in."

"Let me help," I said.

"Not necessary," he insisted, then turned angrily toward the bathroom. "Hey, Yutu—I've got to get in there and your girlfriend's leaving!"

"Coming," he said.

I'm not his girlfriend, you shmendrick, I thought. Why say it? Guys like him didn't hear anything women said anyway.

The bathroom clicked open and Yutu stepped out.

"Aren't you worried about doing business with a guy who won't talk about a freakin' *map*?" I asked the Eskimo.

"I wasn't," he admitted. He looked at Barron. "Should I be?"

"You're both pains," Barron snarled, the alcohol finally showing its ugly face. "I'm gonna clear the air so you'll both stop busting my cojones, all right? You want to know about Fiji? I got sued by an investor who said I didn't deliver what I promised. I caught a break when his Jag went under a big semi hauling a bottom dump trailer. I'm thinking of going back. Lippy's trumpet case? It was a ratty thing that smelled like every sandwich he ever ate off it. You know, Gwen. You saw it. Lippy left before I did. He went one way, I went the other. That's all I know about Lippy and all things Lippy, except for that goddamn song he was humming which made me put my iPod on."

"What song was it?" I asked.

"I don't know, I don't care, and I'm going to tip a kidney," he said, sliding past us. "Then I'm going to get some canvas from storage. Then I'm going to bed. Good night." He closed the bathroom door with a defiant slam.

"Well—that didn't tell me much," I said broodingly.

"I hope you don't consider it a wasted night," Yutu said.

I smiled thinly. There was nothing more fragile— or annoying—than the male ego being needy, unless it's the male ego being belligerent. I didn't consider the night a waste, but I also didn't feel like holding his hand or kissing him good night. What I felt like doing was punching the bathroom door with the side of my fist and asking that tub of seawater—

I strode to the bathroom door and pounded it with the side of my fist.

"What about Tippi?" I yelled.

I heard a flush and then the door opened. "Who the hell is Tippi—and what are you still doing here?"

"Tippi is Lippy's sister," I said.

"You've got to be kidding." Barron smirked. "Are their parents Skippy and Dippy?"

"You're not funny," I said.

"Well, what about her?" Barron asked, appearing genuinely nonplussed.

"Did you kill her or have her killed?" I demanded.

He moved past me, headed toward the door I'd used earlier. "Yutu—get your friend outta here before I call the cops."

"Call them!" I dared. "It's already twelve-twenty and no one in my circle has been arrested yet, far as I know."

Barron turned. "You're crazy. Go. Now."

I stormed toward the exit. "Good night and have a safe trip home," I snapped at a befuddled Yutu White as I went out onto the deck.

"G'night," he said confusedly to the back of my neck as I walked indelicately into the chain, unhooked it, dropped it, and stalked down the plank.

At least now there would be no awkward parting.

Chapter 14

The night was not finished with me.

When I got home, I found Thom sitting on my front stoop. Her head was thrown back and she was looking at the stars. She continued to stare even after I pulled into the short driveway next to her ancient Volvo.

"Is everything okay?" I asked as I hurried over.

She smiled. I didn't like the look of that. It seemed a touch extreme, almost like a birthday party clown. I didn't say anything else until I was right beside her. I sat on the stoop.

"Thom? What are you doing here?"

She turned and leveled that big grin on me. It was definitely not the smile she had when she won a few bucks in Lotto.

"Sitting."

"I can see that—but why?"

"Jesus led me here. I heard his voice when I

turned on the ignition. Then I saw him. There."
She pointed toward my lawn.

"I see," I said. Something was seriously off with
my manager. "Why don't you come inside and tell
me more about it?"

"In a minute." She took one of my hands between hers. "Gwen—do you know what?"

"What?"

She said, "The earth is not happy."

My palm grew sweaty between her cool fingers.
"Who said so?"

"Jesus."

"No," I said. "It wasn't Jesus. You heard Mad say
that."

"Who?"

"Madge Ozenne—the other day, at the deli. She
was sitting with the other Wiccan, Ginnifer. The
woman you knew. Remember?"

"The one who was with the *Satanist*!" she said
with a big, disapproving wheeze.

I froze. When Thom exhaled, I smelled a trace
of alcohol on her breath. That was the biggest
surprise of all. Thom wasn't just a teetotaler, she
was a one-woman temperance movement. That
was one of the reasons she and her husband Otis
split thirty-three years before: she refused to allow
alcohol in her house. Ironically—or intentionally,
or both—Otis, who was career army, later married
a South Korean girl whose father was one of the
nation's leading manufacturers of makkoli, Korean

rice wine. Thom actually showed me a photo of the couple honeymooning on the Sea of Japan near the DMZ. I think she kept it as a way of reminding herself what she had sacrificed for her beliefs. So the idea that she willingly took a drink—

"Out of curiosity," I said, "did you have more than frozen yogurt with Luke and Dani?"

"What? No! I had two T-bird milk shakes at that new place, DesseRt."

A brocha, I thought. That's one of those not-quite-translatable words my Uncle Oskar used to say pretty frequently. It literally means "a prayer" but, depending on the inflection, really means so much more—typically the opposite, that whatever prayer you're planning to say isn't going to help.

"Thom," I said carefully, knowing that this was going to hurt her, "the 'R' is for 'rated adult.' Those drinks are made with Thunderbird—wine."

The poor woman looked like she'd been hit in the face with a sack of matzo brie. She gasped, just guttural sounds, until she could find her voice. "My Lord! My *Lord*!" she wailed. "I have forsaken thee!"

"No," I said. "You didn't know!"

"Oh, God! My God!"

I put my arms around her and held tight. I was going to have some very harsh words with Dani and Luke when I got to the deli. They probably meant well, but Luke had known Thom longer than I had.

They should never have let our resident teetotaler order an alcoholic dessert. Twice.

"Sweet Jesus, I'm a lush!" Thom cried.

"You're not," I said. "You didn't know. It was an *accident.*"

She began to sob. "God will punish me!"

"No, *you* will. And I won't let you do that."

"Oh, God. Then—then I didn't see Jesus under that willow tree?"

"Maybe you did," I said comfortingly. "The two things are probably totally unrelated."

"No, no, no—I'm drunk!"

"It's just the tiniest little buzz," I assured her. I squatted and took her by the arm. "You're blameless. And you're coming inside."

"No, I have to pray. Pray!" she shouted to the stars.

"Fine, but you're doing it inside."

Thom struggled to fold her hands. I let her as she rose unsteadily.

"Our Father, who art in Heaven—forgive me my grave trespass . . ."

Thom was not a tiny woman, but somehow I helped her stand. It wasn't a warm night, but she was perspiring. I honestly didn't think the squirt or two of alcohol had done this to her as much as it released the overpowering guilt and humiliation she felt for everything else that had happened.

She continued to pray, at a faster whisper now, as I opened the door. By the time we got inside she was trembling. She tried to get on her knees but I managed to dump her on the sofa instead. She sat, bent her forehead to her folded hands. I stood to straighten my back. Thom was packed pretty full. *Zaftig,* as they say.

The place still reeked of Aramis, of Dr. Sterne, of the stink of the deal I'd made with him. If I put their bloody hearts on a scale, I didn't know who I disliked more right now: Sterne, his lawyer, or Barron. At least my ex was moving down on the chart. I guess that's progress.

That anything bad should happen to so kind and blameless a person is unconscionable, I thought. Though I wondered obliquely if, in my own way, I'd done something just as stupidly thoughtless to Sally and her coven.

I was too tired to think about that now, or anything else. I got Thom to lie down, took off her shoes—and then she came back to life.

"I'm so ashamed," she said, weeping.

"About what?" I asked softly. I knelt between the sofa and the coffee table.

"Going to prison."

There was a paper napkin from my sandwich still on the table. I gave it to her to blow her nose. "You didn't go to prison," I said. "You went to jail . . . and it was just a holding cell. That's not the same thing."

"It had ugly iron bars and obscene words scratched in the wall and a stainless steel toilet," she said. "And prisoners. It had *prisoners*. That makes it a *prison*. God was punishing me for having judged Tippi."

"Not true," I assured her. Where was she *pulling* that stuff from? "Thom, this has been a long, exhausting day and that's just a couple of teaspoons of bum wine talking."

"You shouldn't say that," she chastised me. "They're not 'bums,' they're called 'homeless persons' or 'unfortunates.'"

"Okay, sorry," I told her. "You need to go to bed now. Me, too. We can discuss circumlocution in the morning."

"Discuss *what*?"

I stopped saying anything. I stood, listened while she mumbled about a *bris* she'd once witnessed—I wasn't so fond of them myself, more for the gawking *tantes* gathered around than for the screaming kid—and when Thom finally shut her eyes, I stood there until I was sure she wasn't getting up again. Her voice got hazy, her lips began to move without speaking, and then she was out.

Exhausted, I went to my own bed to crash.

Which was how I awoke: with a crash.

It was daylight—the clock said five fifty-three—and the sound had come from outside. I was still dressed so I hurried to the window to see what had happened. My fuzzy brain processed the looming presence of K-Two in my driveway. She was just getting out of a red pickup that had seen better days. The sound I'd heard was apparently the tailgate clattering hard when she hit the brakes.

I made my toilette then went to check on Thom.

Who wasn't there. Which I should have realized when I didn't see her car in the driveway, but then it took awhile for me to be fully awake. I tried her cell phone, got no answer, and hurriedly dressed.

I waved to K-Two as I came out the door. She was busy breaking out a big, cushy lawn chair, a boom box, and a book on gardening.

"Thanks for coming," I said as I fished for my keys.

"Thanks for this gig," she said. She handed me a business card with her number on it. "In case you need to reach me," she said.

"Thanks." I tucked it in my jeans—the repository for business cards that ended up reappearing as wadded balls after laundering.

"Is there anything you need me to do?" the mixed martial artist asked.

"Just guard the fort," I said. "I left the door unlocked in case you need to use the bathroom."

"Thanks, but not necessary," she said. "Dr. Sterne said he has a key."

I looked at her. "He's got a key?"

"Yes and he said he'd be here this morning. That's all I was told."

I just smiled tensely at her, got in the car, and headed to the deli—praying everyone else behaved themselves on the road. I was very awake now and very annoyed. Sterne had said he would be in touch today—he hadn't specified where and how. *Gai kukken afen yam*, I thought, remembering what Uncle Oskar used to say when someone was seriously out of line. *Go take a dump in the ocean.*

Thom was at the deli. As I walked in the front door, she was moving through the tables like a human tornado, wiping the tops with a *shpritz* of dish soap from a dispenser and a sponge and elbow grease. She didn't acknowledge me as I entered, just concentrated on her work. I would have let her be except that I knew what she was doing.

I walked over beside her.

"Hey, Thom."

"Hey."

"How long have you been here?"

"Not sure," she said. "Two hours, maybe."

"You want to talk about this?"

"Nothing to talk about," she said without stopping.

"I think there is."

"I did something stupid and immoral," she said. "A whole bunch of things, in fact—"

"One by accident, the others because you're human."

"Doesn't matter," she said absolutely. "I'm mortified by this entire week. I don't know how I'm ever going to atone."

"Don't you think that process is well underway?

You regret what happened, you won't do it again—what else can you do?"

"Beg, on my knees, in church, for God's forgiveness."

"Okay," I said. "So go."

"Just like that? Waltz on out? That would compound my sins."

"What if I didn't give you a choice?" I asked.

She finally looked at me. The change in her demeanor was dramatic. That had hit her hard. "Please don't do that," she practically implored me.

"All right, I won't," I assured her.

"That—that would be terrible," she said.

"I told you I wouldn't."

"My whole life I've been a caregiver. For Otis, when he let me. For your dad and uncle, for Stacie. For the staff. I don't want anyone looking after me."

"Is that what you're mad about?" I asked. "Because you put yourself in the hands of Luke and Dani and it didn't work out?"

She sat heavily in one of the chairs. She seemed more exhausted than sad. "I don't know. I feel like my life has been turned upside down. I was *arrested*, Nash. I had *wine*. I prayed to Jesus this morning and for the first time in my life it didn't make me feel better. I don't know what to do!"

"Hon, you need to give yourself time," I said, as Newt arrived. He was smart enough to wave and keep going toward the kitchen. I held Thom's hand. The sponge in it squished. We both looked at each other and laughed.

Sometimes, all it takes to set the world right is a funny sound and some tiny bubbles.

We were still laughing when Luke arrived. He, too, wisely scooted into the back as Thom and I went about our dining-room prep.

Chapter 15

It was a who's who of "Hey—let's return to the scene of the crime!"

I'm sure it was coincidental, but five of the seven diners who we all remembered being there the morning Lippy was murdered were back. They were all regulars, and maybe the stars had aligned this way before; it's just that I'd never noticed it.

There was our mail carrier Nicolette Hopkins, who was just starting her route, bus driver Jackie and her grease monkey gal-pal, Leigh—Thom tried hard *not* to make a face when they arrived holding hands—Ron Plummer of Plum-Tree advertising, and recording mogul Fly Saucer, who was always trying to find new ways of getting Raylene to notice him.

And there was one thing more to bring that tragic morning back. Lippy's trumpet case.

Nicolette found it in a big brown paper bag

stuffed in her wheelie mail-sack thing, which she left parked outside by the door. She noticed it when she was paying, brought it back inside, and left it on an empty table for two. I took it into my office to call Grant while Nicolette sat at the end of the counter to wait. Resting on the flattened bag, the case sat there like a thing alive, latent with mystery like the monolith in *2001*. I could swear I heard it hissling, like Lippy.

I made the call, then looked the case over. I looked around the side of the lid, didn't see any wires or anything. It *could* have been booby-trapped to explode or release a toxin or something. I took a letter opener from the pencil holder, put the point under the lid, and raised it slowly. Nothing happened. I lifted it completely. The brass hinges made a slight squeaky whine like air being let out from the end of a balloon. I lowered my desk lamp and looked inside.

It was a crappy case, all right. The felt was worn where the trumpet had rested and frayed where it met the wooden boards of the case. I noticed, then, a faint, familiar smell.

The slightly warped top of the case was lined with paper—wallpaper, it looked like and I sniffed around the lid. The smell was strongest in one corner and I felt it; the surface was a little lumpy. I used the letter opener to pick at it. The corner did not yield so I dug harder. It came away, dropping tiny particles of white into the case.

Paste. That was what I had smelled, hidden under the odor of old grapefruit juice. Cheap, five-and-dime white paste. The kind Lippy would buy—if he had bothered to repair the flap. Given the rips and hanging threads elsewhere in the case, I couldn't see why he would have. I looked closer at the underlying wood, which was covered with clumps of paste. I used the letter opener to chip it away. It wasn't old and dry like one of those kindergarten projects with colored paper and macaroni. It still had a waxy quality. Someone had repaired it, and recently. I took a safety pin from my desk drawer and opened it. I used the pin point to gently stab the chunks of paste and remove them. I didn't want to damage the underlying wood in case anything was there. If there was any evidence in the paste itself, like hair or skin, it would still be in the case somewhere when the police lab went over the contents. It just wouldn't be under the flap. I was curious, I had a right to do this, and if Grant didn't like it—well, once again, Uncle Oskar said it best: *Meshuga zol er vern un arumloyfn iber di gasn.* He should go nuts and run through the streets.

I removed a flat, ivory-colored chunk, like a stepped-on piece of feta, and froze. It wasn't on the wood that I found something. It was on the *tuchas* end of one of the paste chunks. Two smudgy blue markings—handwriting, in ink? They looked like "pp." It could have been part of Lippy or

Tippi. A letter for his sister? My mind jumped to words like "happening" and "apparently." Did this have something to do with the treasure he told Tippi about? I looked again at the smear. It could also have been an "rr" that ran. For Barron? I took a picture with my cell phone.

I set the safety pin and the chunk on the felt and looked at the corresponding piece of wood. I couldn't see anything there so I took the magnifying glass from the desk drawer—the one Uncle Murray had used to read fine print. Between safety pins, the magnifying glass, a deck of cards, and a silver dollar, that drawer was more diverse than Batman's utility belt.

There was a very faint indentation in the wood of the lid. I knew at once what it must be and, marking the spot, I closed the lid slowly. That was where the rim of the trumpet bell had pressed up against the lid, which was inwardly warped because its owner was always leaning on it—to eat, to write, to sleep. Maybe Lippy had tucked a piece of paper into what was once a torn-down flap. When the instrument had pressed on it, a trace of wet ink—probably from a felt-tipped pen—had soaked into the porous wood.

Aware that Grant was on the way, I quickly looked up school paste online. The ingredients of cheap paste were water, corn syrup, white vinegar—

"White vinegar?" I said, looking down at the dandruffy felt. I use it to clean stains from the coffee maker. It also cleans grease . . . and newsprint, when that stuff used to get on everything you touched. My great-grandfather Benny bet the horses and read a half-dozen tabloids when New York still had them. The old Frigidaire was always covered with fingerprints.

The vinegar in the paste had picked up the impression of writing that had been crushed into the wood, like Silly Putty picking up a comic-strip picture. Switching on the small scanner I rarely used that was buried under catalogues for clothes and accessories I would never buy, I picked up the pin, gently set the bottom of the paste chunk on the scanner, and made a copy. Then I put it back in the case and removed the pin. If the lab guys noticed the hole—then they noticed the hole. Good for them. Another puzzle to solve.

I used the letter opener to lower the lid so there were no additional fingerprints, then went back to the dining room—just as Grant was entering casually, furtively, so as not to alarm the clientele—if a man holding purple rubber gloves and looking like an OB-GYN on a mission can be called furtive. He acknowledged me with a nod and went to my office. I noticed that neither Leigh nor Fly Saucer was looking at him. Mr. Saucer was focused on his iPad and Leigh was enviously eyeing a vintage Mustang that was parked in the street.

I followed him into the office as soon as I was finished chopping onions.

"Worst evidence locker on earth," he said, bending and looking the case over like a vet examining a sick puppy.

"What do you mean?"

"Any smells that might be on the case are drowned by everything else," he said. "I'll have to take this back to the lab ASAP—check for prints, ascertain that it was even his."

I leaned forward, sniffed. "It was."

"Oh?"

"Lippy spilled grapefruit juice on the case the morning he was killed," I told him. "I know rotten fruit when I smell it."

Grant raised the lid, looked inside, touched the lining here and there. It was badly faded crushed red velvet. "The juice could be how the toxin was introduced. We'll know when we've tested the case. There's a hard spot here," he said, jabbing a spot.

"Meaning?"

"Possibly glued, repaired."

"It's an old case," I said. "He could have done that himself. I'm guessing there are no cameras where the mail bag was left."

Grant grinned crookedly. "This isn't exactly New York, Gwen. We don't have a Ring of Steel."

The detective was referring to the combination

of public surveillance cameras, private security systems, and radiation detectors that effectively watched every foot of Lower Manhattan for roughly a half-mile in all directions from the Financial District.

"So Nicolette could have had it there already—or someone could have put it there," I said.

He glanced at me. "Your eyes are red," he said, awkwardly—okay, painfully—looking for a way to show concern.

"It's the onions," I said truthfully—okay, dismissively.

"I'm going to get an evidence bag," he said. "I'll be back in a minute."

"Okay. I'll be in the kitchen if you need anything else."

"I don't," he answered honestly. Okay, bitterly.

I left, then he left; only the tension remained, the only thing we seemed to have in common. Was this another way hate got itself birthed—not from the axe-chop of a divorce but by the blossoming petals of resentment?

Apparently. That was a new one for me, and even more unpleasant because it was so insidious. It was like the slow, awful awareness of, "Hey—that's not indigestion. It's my *farshtunken* heart!"

I decided to make myself useful; I went to the dining room to see who else might have poisoned Lippy Montgomery.

I picked Fly Saucer because I didn't feel like

dealing with the two ladies. I was sufficiently fed up with men that I was afraid I might hit on them. Not really—but maybe. Then again, thinking about the complex relationship I had with Thom, I wondered if I could actually handle another woman's issues.

Fly was sitting there in his trademark yellow button-down and white slacks, all bald, five-foot-eight of him. He wore Chamber sunglasses with dark ale lenses and a Rolex Deepsea. I have no idea whether he had ever gone diving in his life; but the watch was big and ostentatious, probably so it could compete with the money-green Jesus face and rosary chain he wore tight around his neck. The Christ had tiny diamonds for eyes and lips made of rubies. He seemed to be smiling. Fly had his iPad and was pecking away as he ate.

At least the music mogul made the ice breaking easy. As I walked over with my all-access coffeepot, offering refills, he smiled through his goatee and asked, "What's all the commotion?"

"You mean the police?" I asked, then added my own lame attempt at mock bonding, "The fuzz?"

He grinned after a brief hesitation, then slurred in his best blaxploitation drug dealer voice, "Yeah—*de fuzz*, baby. You so urban."

I meant it as a joke; he was biting back. I guess sarcasm doesn't always work across ethnic lines.

"I was teasing," I said.

He put a fist to his chest, over his heart. "And

brotha Fred Williamson and sista Pam Grier be smiling because they are still-hip jargonauts."

I didn't need this. I wasn't even sure what he'd just said.

I started to leave but Fly grabbed my left wrist with four big rings that happened to be wearing fingers. "Hold on," he said. "That was my turn to be tease-alicious."

I've always had a soft spot for neologists, going back to when my great-relatives from Eastern Europe mangled the local tongue. At least these words had a kind of vitality and ingenuity. Not like the boobs who sent me e-mails about the deli saying our ads had "peaked" their interest or that my food is "kewl."

"Okay," I said.

"So what's up?" he asked, switching on what apparently was meant to be charm.

"Something belonging to Lippy Montgomery just showed up," I told him.

"Is that good? Is there a break in the case?"

For a moment, I thought he was referring to the trumpet case. "I don't know," I said. "I hope so."

"Why? Fuzz-heat on ya?"

He was being sarcastic. "No. I had a soft spot for Lippy."

Fly resumed what he was doing—writing music, it seemed. "He was a damn good horn player. I got him a few sessions—sometimes at the studio, sometimes at The Oatmeal Stallion, but he always did himself in."

The Oatmeal Stallion was the hot jazz club on Union Street. I didn't realize Lippy had ever played that upscale. "How so?"

"He had the soul of a musician, man," he told me. "In the middle of a vocal, he would go off in his own jazz riff world. I understood it, and he was always trying to make something better, but that's not what he was hired to do." There was anger—frustration?—in Fly's voice.

"Did anyone ever get mad at him in those sessions?"

Eerily on cue, Mad Ozenne walked in when I invoked her name. She drifted to the empty table she had occupied the morning of the murder. Her eyes locked on me and stayed with me as she circled wide around the dining room, almost like the moon orbiting the earth. Her expression was equally stony, now that I thought of it. Not angry, just frozen in a blank mask.

"You couldn't get mad at Lippy," Fly said. "Nobody could. He was so sincere and, like I said, it was never about him, about trying to call attention to himself. It was always about the music." He touched his iPad as I topped off his cup. "I read he got poisoned." He raised his tablet slightly. "They find out where or how?"

"Not sure," I said.

"What about his sister?"

"Don't know," I said, unsure whether rat poison had been mentioned in any of the news coverage.

He shook his head slowly. "It's a serious crime."

"Well, yeah. Murder," I said.

"No, man. I mean the way folks just ignored his ass."

"What do you mean?"

"Yo, dude be playing his heart out, nobody giving him a listen. I don't think he cared, 'cause he was out there for himself. But it just wasn't right."

"Why didn't you sign him? If you don't mind my asking."

"'Cause the other thing about Lippy—he had zero charisma. You got to have that if you're gonna record, because you also gotta get out there and support your efforts. Y'know? County fairs, local TV, football halftimes. He had no showmanship. You look at the great trumpeters, like Al Hirt, Doc Severinsen—you want to watch them as much as you want to listen to them."

I saw his point. Lippy was like a herring without the egg and onion. He lacked a certain zest.

"Sad," I said. I leaned in a little. "His sister told me he had some kind of treasure. You ever hear anything about that?"

Fly's mouth pinched like he was rolling coffee grounds from his tongue. "Lippy? Treasure? That boy was so naive he would've tried to return a gold doubloon to Cortez."

That was an unexpectedly literate allusion, I was pleased to note. Maybe the bling boss act was just that.

Before I could say anything more, Leigh waved me over and pointed at her cup. The grease monkey needed more lube. I smiled at Fly and wished him a good day, not sure if there was anything else I could find out from him about Lippy.

And then he offered it himself, again.

"Yo, they oughta talk to that crazy-ass biddy with the teeth tats," Fly said. "I heard her ask him for the pepper."

"Why would she do that when she had some on her own table?"

He shrugged. "Dunno. Maybe it was clogged."

That didn't sound right, but I was already hustling over to fill Leigh's cup—and wondering, with a mind on overload, if there was any socio-ethnic significance to the fact that *yo* and *oy* were mirror images of each other.

"Thank ya, darlin'," she said in a rolling southern welcome that made her sound like Elvis in *Viva Las Vegas* but also sounded like a come-on. Maybe I was wrong. She didn't check me out. I didn't know whether I was pleased or insulted or both.

"How are you ladies today?" I asked.

"Life is good," said Leigh. She was very slender, kind of concave on top, but her bare, freckled arms showed muscle. She wore a baseball cap on her short, red hair. Jackie was a larger woman who strained her blue bus driver uniform. Her platinum blond buzz cut had green tops, like a strange hybrid asparagus.

"Is there anything new about Lippy?" Jackie asked. Her voice was even lower than Leigh's.

"Not really," I said.

"Looks like some new evidence turned up."

We all fell silent as Grant came by. He stopped beside Nicolette, bent over her. We heard him ask her to step out to the car and give him a statement. They left together without a look or a word.

The three of us remained uncomfortably silent. I had gotten a dose of freezer burn from the chill. I had no idea whether the two ladies did or didn't know about me and Grant, but they seemed frozen for a moment.

"Did you guys know Lippy?" I asked as I went to pour, forgetting that I already had.

"Except to hear him tooting in the distance, no," Leigh said.

"He rode my bus a couple times a week," Jackie said.

"Well, there ya go," Leigh said. "That's why I wouldn't've known him. PTG—public transport guy. He would have had no need of my services."

"Any of them," Jackie winked.

"Dawg," Leigh fake snarled.

Oy.

"Y'know, it's strange about Lippy," Jackie said, mercifully getting back on point. "He looked lonely but he never acted like he was missing out on anything. He was always busy with something."

"Like what?" I asked.

"Fussing with his instrument, mostly," she said. "Smiling to himself. Reading a newspaper or magazine he picked up off a seat. He'd spread it out on his trumpet case like it was a feast. He didn't seem unhappy." Then she said, "Sometimes he would sit there writing on a yellow legal pad."

I came alert, like *shtetl* dwellers hearing hoof beats. "What did he write?"

"I don't know. Writing."

"Was he intense or kind of casual?"

Jackie rolled her shoulders as she swallowed coffee from her refilled mug.

"How'd you see all that, drivin'?" Leigh asked.

"I stop at lights, check around," Jackie said. "I also look back when people make sounds that could mean trouble. My job is more than just steering a wheel."

"You're so capable, you multitasker," Leigh cooed.

Meh keyn brechen as Uncle Oskar used to say. *You could vomit from this.* Public lovebirding of any persuasion is not for me. So was the next thing.

"But I couldn't do what poor Tippi could in *Cirque de So Laid*," Jackie said soberly.

I jerked so hard the coffee sloshed in the pot. "What?"

"Her first adult film," Leigh said. "We did a

minimarathon, watched all three of her movies the other night when we read about her death. That girl could—contort."

"Lippy was actually in one of them," Jackie said.

"*What?*" This conversation had seriously stunted my vocabulary.

"The movie was called *Come Blow Your Horny*," Leigh explained. "It was set in the 1950s. Lippy was playin' horn in a jazz club where Tippi was workin' as a cigarette girl by night, an exotic hooker by later at night. It was her last picture, according to the AFCACDB."

"The AFCA—what?"

"The Adult Film Cast and Crew Database," she said. "The other one was called *Lifeguard on Judy*, in case you want to download them," Jackie added. "That was more of a period piece, heavy on the—"

"I get the picture," I cut her off.

"It was during her red period," Leigh snickered.

"Literally," Jackie added.

"Hey, I've got to get back to work," I said, backing away with a sense of urgency.

I turned to go, Leigh and Jackie tucked back into their breakfasts, and I wondered what Lippy could possibly have written, then torn from a pad and tucked into the ripped flap of his case . . . and whether that could in any way qualify as a "treasure." Something that Robert Barron or someone else found out about and would want. Then I remembered what Fly had said about Mad, who happened to be sitting right where I was facing. I looked down at her and she looked up at me and there was a moment of awkward silence. Her expression was still noncommittal, but I had a feeling she wasn't quite a blank slate. We had unfinished business, and this was another rare morning visit.

"Hello, Mad," I said.

"Not happy," she said.

"I know," I said. "The earth can take a number and stand in line. Listen, Mad, I'm truly sorry about what happened at the house and I want to figure out a way to make things right. But I have to ask you something. On the morning he died, did you ask Lippy Montgomery—he was sitting right there, at the counter—did you ask him for pepper?"

"I did not," Mad said with a strange mix of certainty and innocence.

"Someone says they heard you."

"They're mistaken."

"You didn't speak with him at all?" I asked.

"I did speak to him," Mad said.

"What did you say?" I asked. I would have described this Q&A as "pulling teeth," only in Mad's case the metaphor didn't quite apply.

"I asked him about the paper," Mad said.

I thought back. I didn't remember a newspaper, but he may have picked one up on the bus. "Did Lippy give you a newspaper? Was there something marked on it? Circled? An ad or something?"

The Wiccan looked away, stared straight ahead.

I couldn't tell if she was being passively belligerent or was just being her usual, oblivious self.

"Mad, everything that happened while Lippy was here is important," I pressed. "Isn't there *anything* you can tell me?" *And please don't tell me "the earth isn't happy," or I can't be responsible for what happens to the coffeepot.*

"Yes," Mad said thoughtfully. "May I order now?"

Chapter 16

I left Mad humming some witchly sounding ditty as I left the dining room for the sane, controlled security of my office.

Putting aside the necessity of making a living, there are many, many reasons why a person goes into a particular profession.

They might love it—an actor, for example, or a bake shop owner. A journalist, maybe.

They might be expected to go into it—a family business or a family trade, like the *shmatta* business—literally the "rag" business but only euphemistically. Your father made shirts, you made shirts. Your father imported bulk cloth from Taiwan, you sold bulk cloth from Taiwan. That didn't hold true for women in my culture; your father repaired shoes, you married a heart surgeon.

Some people go into a line of work because they want to serve the public good, they want power, they like a challenge, they want to serve God—the reasons and choices go on and on.

Occasionally, someone takes a job to radically change their life. To transfer to another country, put their shoulder against a new challenge. A subset of that is to flee an old life, to palate cleanse, which was my reason. Not that choosing to be an accountant had been driven by anything profound; it was an interesting enough field with plenty of opportunity, a glass ceiling that had enough cracks for me to rise, and a chance to meet what my grandmother called "a fella." I was lucky. At the time when my life was in shambles, when Wall Street became so scandal-ridden that it was less embarrassing to admit to porn semi-stardom, the opportunity to take over Uncle Murray's deli came along. I grabbed it like it was the last chocolate creme–filled donut on the shelf.

Now, a year later, came the self-analysis: While it was the right move, did I want it to be a permanent move? Was I happier than I was a dozen months ago? Yes. Lonelier? About the same. More optimistic? I'm a Jew. That doesn't apply.

Every time I went into the office to place orders for supplies, it was a weird collision of careers, a mix of deli needs and financial savvy. It was the time I liked the least, since it took me back mentally and emotionally to the *other* time. And yet—

Today was different. With Grant giving me the cold beef shoulder and the Wiccans probably casting spells and the school about to chop up my home and my anchor Thom lost in a psychological Mariana Trench, not to mention the lingering weirdness of the Barron-Candy run-in, plus a message from Yutu thanking me for a great going-away present, which it wasn't, it was more like an I've-got-nothing-to-do-right-now-so-this-will-fill-the-time-nicely—I felt emotionally and physically exposed and was beginning to yearn for the comforting anonymity of New York, where even the sexually "out" folks were comfortably casual about their lifestyle instead of in your face. New York, where I hadn't known my father had a long-time love affair with a crazy lady. New York, where my ex had the good manners to just fade away. New York, where I had never found a dead body in my backyard or accidentally fed an acquaintance a fatal dose of poison or had a man fall through the ceiling into dinner.

Was it time to get the hell out of Nashville? Or was I missing the point of everything that had happened? Should I embrace it and never let go? Because, whatever else could be said about my one-year anniversary, I had learned more about myself and faced more growth-inducing challenges than I had in the first three-plus decades of my life combined.

And yet, I thought, *there was probably a limit to how many tidal forces a person could endure.*

I wasn't sure I was designed for this kind of

exponential growth. Or if it was necessary or even healthy. There was something to be said for sameness, for limitations. Everyone who spoke of Lippy, for example, mentioned that he seemed to be secure in his own world. I could have been, in New York, with a small accounting practice.

I think.

That was the problem. One could never know and, in any event, nothing was ever perfect. And here I was.

"What the hell *are* you doing here?" I asked myself. A desk full of papers and folders, a drawer full of *tchochkes*, a dining room full of strange people, and a life full of people I wished were somewhere else.

I had no answer. But here I was, and I wasn't one to cry about things I could change if I chose to.

Even though Lippy's trumpet case had only been there a few minutes, the office felt naked and spacious without it. That poor, flimsy thing had history; it had weight. And it probably had a message for whoever was clever enough to figure it out.

I looked at the scan I had made of the bit of paste, blew up the image, rotated it, and saw nothing new in it. I e-mailed the image to myself so I could look at it later and turned to the daily inventory. I went to the kitchen, counted. We were low on carrots and cabbage for the coleslaw, low on onions—which made me think of Grant's dopey comment—low on Diet Coke and low on coffee. That was probably my fault. I was drinking enough to float a horseshoe, as I once overhead someone say down here.

Lunch came and went in a blur. When it was over, I did something I'd been putting off: I called K-Two to see how things were going. To my surprise, they weren't.

"No one from the university showed," she said.

"Did anyone call?"

"Not a soul. I've been sitting here tailgate-watching videos on YouTube—oh, I used some of your outside juice. I hope you don't mind."

It took me a moment to figure out that she meant electricity. If you work in a restaurant long enough, words like "juice" and "fried" only have one meaning.

"That's fine," I told her. "So no one's been there all day?"

"Just a Cherokee lady on a motorcycle," K-Two said. "Said her name was Sally. She had a cat with her, in a basket. She let the cat out—it ran off and I haven't seen it since—and then she put something in your mailbox."

My stomach gurgled. "Was it a letter?"

"I guess," K-Two said. "What else?"

"Something dead," I said. "Would you mind taking a look?"

"Glad to. Don't really feel like I earned my pay today."

K-Two hummed as she walked to the curb. I'd heard the melody before.

"What's that you're humming?" I asked.

"I don't know. A song."

"Did you hear it on YouTube?"

"Maybe," she said. I heard the mailbox door squeak. "It's a business envelope. Typed. Just your name on it. Return address is—Trial of Tears Law Offices, PO Box 602206B, Nashville. Want me to open it?"

"Sure," I said.

"Hold on." She hummed again as she slit the envelope. "It says—oh, this is interesting."

"What is?" K-Two was exasperating. It was both a testament to our culture, and fortunate for our citizens, that there was a place in the world for this woman.

"It's not addressed to you but to Andrew A. Dickson III, Esquire," she said. "This is a cc."

K-Two proceeded to read what I pretty much expected to hear: that my house was now a temple and that no "desecrating hands, feet, or souls" would be permitted access to the grounds for any purpose other than "prayer and the worship of the mother," which I took to mean the earth. The one who was not happy. It further stated that a representative of the Cherokee people, Mrs. Sally Biglake, would

be camping on the property when her familiar—
Little Pie—had disbursed any rats and evil spirits.

"It's signed Joseph M. Bushyhead," K-Two con-
cluded.

I once read about a pig, in Medieval France,
that was arrested and put on trial for murder. So
I'm not sure that this situation was unprecedented
in the history of jurisprudence. But it was definitely like nothing I'd ever encountered. And it
also meant—apparently—that I was not just going
to be relocated because of a yearlong dig, I was
about to be displaced permanently.

"So—does this letter say that the biker chick
owns your home?"

"That seems to be the claim," I told her.

"Wow. At least you can sleep at your deli, right?"

"Yeah Right there on the counter. I'll use the
paper towel dispenser for a pillow."

"Why don't you just bring one from here?"
K-Two asked.

I smiled at the phone. Sometimes, God sends
humor at just the right moment.

And sometimes, God sends that *loch in kop*.

Nicolette Hopkins came back after finishing
her mail route and asked to see me alone. I invited her back to the office. The little room no
longer seemed empty. Nicolette was a smallish

woman, the classic five-foot-two, eyes-of-blue, albeit with some miles on the chassis. The longest conversation we'd ever had was at Christmas when I gave her twenty bucks. She told me she was a single mother, that her job was in jeopardy due to USPS downsizing, and that her union was worthless. The only thing I hadn't known was about the kid, an eight-year-old boy who was a hell raiser.

"I just wanted to tell you, I think Detective Daniels is angry," she said. "At you."

Nicolette was now three-for-four telling me things I already knew.

"Why do you say that?" I asked.

"He asked if anything was loose in the case when I found it. I told him I didn't think so."

"Oh," I said. *Oops*, I thought.

"Did you open it?" she asked.

I said evasively, "Why would I?"

She nodded. "That's what I told him. He didn't seem to buy that."

"Well, something could have jogged loose when I moved it from the counter," I said. "Hey, neither of us asked for this to drop in our laps—or in our mail bag, right?"

She nodded, though she was obviously unhappy to be part of a criminal investigation. Like many of the people I'd met down here, Nicolette seemed to be a sort of down-home type who was happy to go through her day—her life—without any kind of high drama. Or homicide.

"You were here that morning," I went on. "Did you see anything unusual?"

"Besides Mad?"

"Do you know Mad?" I asked. I had felt compelled to ask that; I didn't like snap judgments about people based solely on the way they looked or dressed. We were all a little strange to someone.

As it turns out, Nicolette had every reason to judge Mad.

"I know her," the fortysomething woman told me. "My ex-husband Samson owned the tattoo parlor where she and the other witches did their body art. One of the women wanted eyes on her eyelids. Sammy did it—but some ink dripped in the corner of one eye. It got infected and she lost her sight."

"Ginnifer," I said.

Nicolette nodded. "It was kind of a hobby for Sammy. I was the breadwinner and he was not a very good businessman. He hadn't paid the insurance. It cost us everything to settle the debt and pay our lawyer. Sammy was so ashamed he ran off. I never got to tell him I was pregnant."

"Jesus!"

Nicolette was suddenly embarrassed. She turned away. "I shouldn't be troubling you with all this—"

"It's no trouble," I assured her. "A fire in a saucepan—*that's* trouble."

"Thanks," she smiled. She was tearing up and I fished the tissue box from under my inventory clipboard. I extended it toward her. She yanked one out and blew her nose. "Jesus," the woman said bitterly. "Sammy was MIA. But Mad was not. The other morning, when I saw her here? I almost left. But I didn't want to let her impact my life—again."

"What happened between you?"

"Sammy swore he warned Ginnifer that tattooing her eyelids wasn't the best idea in the world," Nicolette said. "Mad was there when he told her—but when we had her deposition, she said he never told them anything."

"Were you there?"

"I was on my route," Nicolette said. "But Sammy talked about it over dinner the night he did it, told me he told them how nuts it was."

"Then why did he do it?" I asked.

"Because Sammy liked a challenge. He was an artist, not a brain surgeon."

Or an ophthalmologist, I thought. "I assume you've tried to contact him."

"I tried hard," she said. "As soon as I had some money, I hired a private detective. He traced Sammy as far as Bristol, then lost him in the Appalachians. I figure he must be up there, somewhere, living a life without lawyers, without witches, without electricity. He's probably holed up in a cave somewhere, making his own paints and doing, like, prehistoric art." I was still holding the tissue box. She took another. "I just wish he could see his son and his son could see him. How's that for a life's ambition?"

"Sounds pretty good, actually." I was thinking of my own father blowing out of New York and making minimal effort to see me for the rest of his days. I palmed a tissue as I put the box back on my desk.

"I should go," Nicolette said. "I'm glad I came back. I hope none of that stuff with the trumpet case gives you any trouble."

"It won't," I assured her. "We were just being good citizens."

I felt a little bad lying to her, but the trumpet case was a passing thing. I would see Nicolette every day. I didn't want her to think I was a pushy New Yorker who would insert herself where she didn't belong—even though I sort of was. It's something most Nashvillians wouldn't understand.

I dried my own eyes and ignored the private line when I saw that it was Grant calling. If he had a professional beef, he could take it up with me officially, in person. I wasn't going to give him a convenient opportunity to transfer his frustration with me to whatever he thought I did with the case. I had this perverse fantasy that Grant and Reynold Sterne would show up at the same time and beat each other's brains out in an effort to get to me.

I left the office and went to see how Thom was. As I walked toward the counter, I heard something that surprised me.

A lot.

Chapter 17

The bathroom was off the wall opposite my office. As I walked toward the dining room, Luke was walking the other way. He was an aspiring musician who played local gigs with his band, the Gutter Crickets, whenever he could get them.

As he passed, he was singing a song I recognized.

"Whoa," I said, turning as he passed.

"Huh?"

That exchange was crudely monosyllabic, even by Luke's and my standards.

"That song—what is it?"

"'More Coffee,'" he said.

"That's the name of it?"

He nodded. "It starts out slow and then gets wild."

"I see. This is the third time I heard it recently," I told him. "Where did *you* hear it?"

"On the radio," Luke said. "It's the new one by Ximene, the Spanish electric harpist. It's gonna be a big, big hit."

That would explain it, then. Why everyone seemed to know it but me. When I listened to music, it was usually sugary, romantic-era piano—Chopin, Liszt, Mendelssohn, Beethoven. That was also what I had played, in truncated dumbed-down form, during the three years I endured piano lessons. "Für Elise." "The Spring Song." "The Minute Waltz." I wasn't a snob, I just didn't like breaking in new stuff . . . or listening to lyrics. I heard enough words during the course of the day. Still, a harp didn't sound so bad. So far, today, I had a new tune and new porn added to my mental Netflix-iTunes repository.

I thanked Luke for the information and continued on my way.

I could tell that Thom's engine was running down. Usually, if there was no one to seat or no bill being paid, she would refill the toothpick dispenser, add mints to the bowl beside the cash register—the one with the little spoon no one ever used; for some unholy reason, people just dug in with their fingers—or make sure the laminate menus were free of ketchup, coffee, or pickle-juice stains.

She was just standing there, looking vacantly into the dining room. Granted, she had been here since early morning and had hit the tiles running.

But this look was something different. It spoke of an inner exhaustion. I'd seen that in my mother toward the end of her life, and that concerned me. Mom wasn't that much older than Thom when she died. Granted, my mother had packed a lot of disappointment into a steady decline. She'd managed the women's outerwear department for Gimbels in Herald Square. Mom had loved the retailer so much that she actually collected postcards of the area that showed the big blue and yellow store sign. Some of my own earliest memories were of running in and out of the circular clothes racks with my childhood friend Alice. My mother wept for days when the chain went broke in 1987. When her marriage went bust, she bootstrapped herself into survival mode and held a variety of jobs in retail. But she was never the same not exactly happy but content woman I remembered. She grew thin, the lines in her face deepened with more than age, her eye sockets blackened in a way that sleep couldn't erase. It was almost as if she carefully, methodically laid the groundwork for the heart attack that took her in her sleep at age fifty-nine.

Thom wasn't much younger than that. She didn't have the kinds of stresses that my mother had allowed to pile on and Thom, at least, could push some of them off onto Jesus. But I recognized the thousand yard stare. An explosion of violence, a release of pent-up rage, followed by an arrest—that could be as traumatic to a God-fearing Southern Baptist churchgoer as a retail store closing was to a New York Jewish woman.

"Hey," I said, approaching the checkout counter. "No daydreaming on the job."

Thom rolled her eyes toward me like a Kewpie doll. "I'm not daydreaming. I'm thinking."

I said in a conspiratorial whisper, "You're setting a bad example for employees who *don't* think. If I let Newt stare into space, fries will crisp. If I let A.J. or Dani stare into space, the Cozy Foxes will go unfed."

Thom's eyes shifted to the group of women sitting in the corner. She lifted and lowered her broad shoulders.

"So? They take up a big table for hours while they talk about their mysteries, only ordering free coffee refills."

"It's good community relations," I pointed out. "And it's good for passersby to see people at the tables. Folks don't like to eat alone, or think the food is *drek*."

The big eyes shifted back to me. "You're right. I know. I'll get to work."

"No, what you'll do," I said, "is work on getting over what happened. Standing there thinking about it isn't going to do you any good."

"I was praying," she said.

"You weren't," I said. "Your lips move when you pray."

"They do?"

"Just a little," I smiled. I leaned in a little closer. "You did it. It happened. You learned. If you hold onto anything but the last part, you'll keep reliving the misery. Isn't that what hell is? Do you really think you, of all people, deserve to be there?"

She looked at me with surprise. "Gwen Katz, that was practically—"

"Rabbinical?" I asked.

"I was going to say pontifical, but yes, that would be more appropriate."

I smiled. "I took a philosophy course in college and one of the few things that made an impression was the idea that the door to hell is locked from the inside. I'm not going to let you stay there. Get the Windex."

Her eyes went wide.

"Back on the horse," I said. "There's a new bottle under the counter—I put it there myself. Get it and clean."

Slowly, like one of those Disneyland robots, Thom bent and picked up the plastic bottle and the roll of paper towels. She held the neck of the bottle as though it were a cobra, a mortal enemy.

And then her lips moved. I could swear she said, "Get thee from me Satan." And she smiled—not just her mouth, but her entire face. And finally she started cleaning. She looked at me, still smiling, and nodded.

The world was back on its axis.

For about a minute.

A short, bulldog of a man whom I did not know walked in, asked me for me, and I told him he'd found me. He handed over an envelope that had my name ink-jetted front and center and the address for the Court for the Middle District of Tennessee on the upper left.

"It's a summons," the man said.

"Too bad," I replied. "The word 'subpoena' stamped in red spoiled your surprise."

He made a face that looked like a big white raisin. "Hey, I only wanted to be sure you understood, lady," he growled. "Some folks can't read."

"They're lucky," I remarked.

I saw, eyeball left, Thom look like she wanted to spray the man. I eased myself between her Windex and the process server as he tipped his baseball cap and left. I sighed and, making sure Thom had calmed again, I walked back to my office, where I slit the envelope with my finger and got a paper cut. I put my finger in my mouth and removed the document inside. It was a yellow piece of paper with what I assumed was the handwriting of Andrew A. Dickson III demanding that I come to court the following morning at ten a.m., prepared to produce any and all documents pertaining to the ordination of my home as a Church of the Wiccan Faith, Nashville Coven.

"Well, that will be easy," I thought.

All I had were some melted candles and an apple skin. I should probably bring those.

What an unmitigated shande, I thought. That means disgrace. The whole thing, from the strong-arm tactics of my Wiccan sisters to the stronger-arm tactics of the university and its tool, the court system. It wasn't a question of who was right and who was wrong; we'd all made mistakes. The question was, who the hell was on my side except for Thom and her Windex bottle?

K-Two, I thought—until I got a text from my personal superhero saying that she was going to leave because Dr. Sterne was no longer paying her—at least, not until this issue was resolved. That was just lovely. I thought about paying her myself, but then I wouldn't sleep counting the money I was wasting. So I would be home alone tonight with Sally Biglake camped on my lawn, her demon-hunting cat prowling through the bushes, and my two fraidy cats deep under the sofa. Having Grant in my bed was starting to look good again. Or maybe I should just break another of Robert Barron's portholes and stay with him.

I helped here and there with the late afternoon stragglers, then gave Newt, Luke, and Dani a hand with the closing. I cleaned the slicer. There was something relaxing about that task. Sharp and shiny metal things got unscrewed, put in a sink full of hot water, scrubbed, then reassembled all gleaming and fresh. If only we could do that to ourselves.

There was, at least, a kind of spring-renewal type of vibe to be gleaned from Luke and Dani, who were dating. When the twenty-two-year-old Lady Gaga wanna-be came in for the afternoon shift, Luke brightened. When they left together, they were off to see the infamous CreepLeeches, whose van we'd borrowed for our first catering event, the one that had been spoiled a little by the death of a partygoer. The cynic in me couldn't help but wonder how long the relationship would last. But the twenty-two-year-old buried in my brain remembered that time of life and was buoyed by their innocence.

I kicked Newt out—he could finish swabbing the walk-in freezer in the morning—and Thom and I walked down the street to the garage.

"Thanks for today," she said as we started out.

"C'mon, there's no need for that," I said. "We do for each other."

"I know. But I forget sometimes how much you've taken on, what the learning curve was, how strange it all is for you—not just having to run a business and support a very needy staff, but also just being down here." She reached into her shoulder bag and took out a small gift-wrapped box. "Anyway, this is for your one-year anniversary.

May there be many, many more. And I say that selfishly."

I took the box but I looked at her. I wasn't expecting this. I'm sure it showed and I literally didn't know what to say. Fortunately, with Thom, it wasn't always necessary to say anything. I just cradled the box and we walked arm in arm to our cars and we said good-bye with a long, tight hug.

"Don't stress too much about the legal stuff," Thom said. "God is the final judge."

"True, and I have to confess I'm happier not to be facing him tomorrow."

"Whenever you do, the gates of heaven will open wide," Thom said confidently.

I wasn't sure I'd get through the Pearly Gates, what with the Commandments I'd busted over the years, but I did open the box when I got in the car. It was a tall white coffee mug that said "I ♥ New York" on one side and "I ♥ Nashville" on the other. There was a little handwritten card inside that said, *Whatever you feel on any given day, you can drink from that side. All my love and God bless you, T.*

I sat in the car and cried for a long couple of minutes.

Chapter 18

The noise from the den pulled me from a restless sleep.

I got home about seven-thirty. I'd had a salt and goo craving and stopped at a local pizza place off the highway to pick up a small pie with extra white cheese, onion, mushrooms, and anchovies. I only ate a slice and a half when I got home; seeing Sally's bike at the curb and her small tent in the backyard made me a little queasy. That wasn't typically my reaction to things—loss of appetite— but then I'd never felt so adrift. In a leaky boat. With piranha. And storms always on the horizon. I also had never been the self-pitying type. But you don't realize how much you hold on to "home" and the familiar things around you until they aren't there. And now the place where I lived, which was nominally my home, was being threat- ened. I say "nominally" because I'd never gotten

around to personalizing it. The place still had
Uncle Murray in almost every decorating choice:
functional and mostly secondhand. I'd gotten rid
of almost everything when I left New York. Only
the bed was new and that still had Grant's ghost all
over it.

And speaking of ghosts—

I'd fallen asleep on the sofa during the evening
news and then had dragged my rag-doll body into
the bedroom. I'd conked out solidly until about
midnight, when I awoke with a yelp. I hadn't seen
the cats since I got home and fed them, and now
they were slinking upwards, across my torso, like
doughboys under barbed wire.

I flung them off with a wave of the covers, and
they compromised by settling on the unoccupied
side of the bed. I did the nightly lavatory chores
which I hadn't bothered with earlier, then went
back to bed—for about a half-hour. My brain was
working on the court appearance I hadn't even
prepared for. I awoke feeling tense, managed to go
back to sleep by disassembling and reassembling
the slicer in my head, then woke with a start at
two a.m. when I heard a noise. The cats must have
heard it, too; they were gone.

The noise had come from downstairs through
what was clearly an open door—and the door had
not been opened by me. I kept it shut as a matter
of course because the oil burner rumbled like a
wounded hippo whenever it came on . . . or what I

imagined a wounded hippo would sound like. This
noise was not the oil burner, it was more like a
thump, like a sack of potatoes hitting the floor.
That was a sound I *had* heard, at least.

My first thought was that Sally had come into
the house and gone into the "temple" to pray. But
she didn't have a key and I imagine I would have
heard her kicking open the door or even jimmying
the lock. I went in to the bathroom, which had a
window that looked out on the backyard. It was too
dark to see anything, but everything looked calm
around the small portable camping tent—the kind
all those Occupy loons used. The flap was shut,
something it didn't seem she'd have done if she'd
planned to go back soon.

I heard the sound again. Then I heard smaller
sounds that seemed closer but of the same kind:
thumping or drumming. I considered calling
911 but I didn't just in case it was Sally's cat
having found a way in. The den connected to the
basement-level garage and had a window. My cats
were indoor cats, so who knew what way in her
little witchly "familiar" might have found.

I pulled my bathrobe from the plastic hook
behind the door and picked up a crowbar I kept
behind the door for such moments. It was a practice I'd started in New York, where I never actually
needed to use it. I tiptoed out—though why I did
that I don't know, since it would have been a good
thing to make noise and scare an intruder off.

When you try to walk quietly at night—something I hadn't had to do since I was in high school—floors make noises they never make during the day.

The stairs to the basement were at the opposite side of the house, in the kitchen. I felt a chill as I moved along the hallway that opened into the living room, as though the temperature of the house had been lowered here. I knew it was just me being anxious. The front door came into view and I was relieved to see that it was closed. Which, again, meant nothing. There was still a back door and a garage door.

I jumped when the oil burner came on. I also swore, since now I wouldn't be able to hear any noise coming from the den except that. I shuffled quickly in my bare feet to the kitchen, determined to prevent whoever might be down there from using that noise to cover their escape. I knew my way in the dark and did not turn the light on. There was no reason to make myself visible yet.

The door was indeed open wide. My heart was pumping hard enough to fill my chest front to back as well as up and down. The den light switch and the oil burner switch were on the wall to my left. I threw the light on. I had a limited view of the den from there and I stood, frozen, waiting for something to appear.

It didn't. I went down a step, holding the crow-bar like a baseball bat. I could swear the wooden steps were made of rubber, considering how much

I felt them give. At about this point, I was thinking maybe I should have "Jewish lightning" strike the house, like my mother's cousin Norm did. He torched his paper goods factory after a misprint caused 100,000 Passover Haggadahs to be marked with the year 5762 instead of 5752. Ironically, that was the year Norm ended up getting out of prison.

But burning down my house—which I had no intention of doing—would be a surrender to the many forces battling over the place. I'd lose, too. It would be a relief, but scorched earth was how my father handled things, not me.

I ventured down another step and then I saw it.

It was squatting in the open door to the oil burner room. A figure, in shadows, in what looked like a dark suit. It was standing behind several large bags of salt that I used in the old water softener—hence, the thumps. They had been stacked in a small pile, like sandbags at a rising river.

I turned and ran back up the stairs, slammed the door, and went to the wall phone. It went dead before the 911 operator could pick up—along with the rest of the electricity in my house.

The circuit breakers were located in the oil burner room. Time to get the hell out.

I tucked the crowbar under my arm and ran. My cell phone was recharging on the coffee table. I got to it easily in the dark, grabbed my bag next to it, and with the charger cord dangling behind me, I bolted from the house.

And ran right into someone who blew something up into my face that caused me to back up, gag, and pass out.

I woke with the smell of burned milk in my nose. I've smelled it often enough in neglected pots on the deli burners. I blinked away the dopiness in my brain as I looked out on dim, dim blueness. At first I thought it was the twilight sky, but then I heard crickets. They were right there, under the ringing in my ears.

I tried to get up but my elbows were like dough. I looked to the right and saw Sally in candlelight. She was gazing down at me like my mother used to when I was sick. Sally was on her knees with her hands across her white Nashville Kangaroos sweatshirt. The Roos were a sports team that played some kind of football or soccer—I never bothered to find out which.

"It's Aussie rules football," Sally said.

"Huh?" I looked away; the whiteness of the shirt hurt my eyes.

"The shirt, the Roos," she said. "You looked like you were trying to remember what they were."

"Right. Yeah." I finally crinkled my nose at the smell. "What's going on?"

"I found you passed out on the front lawn," she said. She noticed my gaze shift to a bowl on the left.

"Burned milk," she added. "It clears away evil humors."

"I can see how that would clear a room," I said.

Sally smiled benignly. That was where she broke from my mother. Mom always took good care of me, but under the attention was a critical mouth that said, without actually saying it, *Didn't I tell you not to go out without your scarf?* or *Didn't I tell you not to play with Genie so soon after she had the measles?*

"What were you doing outside?" Sally asked.

"Someone was inside," I said. I remembered my bag, tried to see where it was.

"I have your bag and phone here," she said. "Also, your crowbar."

I thanked her. I was still muddled. She sounded sincere and her ministrations seemed earnest, but this was the same woman who somehow made a bat fly into my window and sent me a legal letter that very afternoon. And was camped on my property. And had the kind of knowledge to prepare dust or powder or whatever it was that got puffed into my *punim* that put me on my back. For all I knew, it had been Sally in my basement.

"How did you know I was out front?" I asked.

"I heard the screen door slam."

"You didn't see anyone?"

"Not a soul," she said.

I didn't know which definition applied. "Do you have any idea what was done to me?"

"Powdered belladonna, I suspect," the woman

said softly, as if she was describing a nice bath oil. "It causes extreme light sensitivity and unconsciousness. In anything larger than the dose you apparently received, it is typically fatal."

"Nice." My mind went right to Tippi's murder, though that was rat poison.

"Who had access to your home?" she asked.

It didn't take me long to answer. "Reynold Sterne has a key."

"And a reason to want you dead and make it appear as though I did it," Sally added.

Even my muddled brain grasped that. What it couldn't accept was that the damn dig was important enough to kill for, especially since the court hadn't even ruled on the matter.

"I should call the cops," I said. "File a report. Have them check for evidence."

"All right, Sister Gwen," she said.

She handed me my cell phone. I'm not sure whether it was my haziness or Sally or both, but she seemed downright creepy. I switched the phone on, the light blazed into the backs of my eye sockets, and I looked away.

"Shall I call for you?" Sally asked.

"What time is it?" I asked.

"Nearly three."

By the time they arrived and left it would be nearly four. Still, there was a possibility that this could be useful. I was getting an idea, probably a bad one, but I was too exhausted to think it through.

"If you wouldn't mind dialing, I'd appreciate it," I said.

I heard the three beeps and she handed me the phone. I told the dispatcher my emergency and gave her my address. She asked me if I was presently still in danger, if the intruder was still in the house. I told her no and I didn't think so. She said a car was already on the way.

Not, I hoped, with Grant Daniels in it.

Grant didn't come, probably because he was off duty and sanely asleep. Two young cops did, both of them in their twenties, I'd say. I was on my feet by then, waiting at the curb. They asked if I needed medical assistance and since I fell back while assuring them I was fine, they called for an ambulance.

While Sally and I waited for the paramedics, the officers went inside. They returned just as the outsourced Nashville HealthBus was finishing up with me. The older medics—one a female nurse, the other a retired doctor, I guessed from the white hair and casual country GP manner—gave me oxygen, checked my vitals, looked into my eyes and nasal passages, and said I was fine unless I felt I needed watching. I told them I didn't. At my request, the physician did take a swab from each nostril and sealed it in a little plastic bag for analysis.

The police found no sign of forcible entry, no trace of displaced salt bags, no footprints on the slated entryway, nothing wrong with the fuse box—only the cats in the bathtub as mute evidence of the home invasion. They looked at me, now, as though they suspected I'd been on some kind of acid trip. Or maybe mushrooms, since they regarded Sally with some skepticism as well.

They radioed in their findings, reserved any opinions they had for their written report, and left shortly after the ambulance did.

"Well, that was productive," I said.

"Did you expect it to be otherwise?"

"No." That was the truth. But it's also how I had always done things: don't get involved. Let the infrastructure handle it, whether it was neighbors arguing or someone smoking in the bathroom at school or someone who dumped personal trash on a public street. You never knew who was homicidal.

But here, now, was the first time I ever felt like I was the one who'd done something wrong.

It began to drizzle. I was too tired and chilly to question Sally further or protest her being here or worry about how things would go in the morning. I just needed to sleep.

Sally helped me in, the cats hissing from the bathroom as we entered the bedroom. I set the alarm for eight—to give myself enough time to gather whatever papers I needed, not that I had very many—then left Thom a message on the deli voice mail saying that I wouldn't be in until after the hearing.

The next thing I knew, I was dreaming about anchovies trying to claw their way from the deep fryer as my father slammed the wire mesh basket down on them . . .

I was up like a hen at cockcrow, alert and not sure what to expect. I'd either be laying eggs or getting what my chicken-raising great-great-grandmother called *tashmesh* and I just called a screwing.

I grabbed my papers, did some quick online research as I had coffee and a raisin bagel, and made it to the court with thirty seconds to spare, traffic at this hour being very different from the traffic I was accustomed to ninety minutes earlier in the day. The hearing was held in a small room at One Public Square and it was pretty much what I had expected, a complete waste of my time. It was a pair of attorneys arguing through me—or rather with me as a shuttlecock. Andrew A. Dickson III was at one table, Joseph M. Bushyhead, a Cherokee, was at another, and I was on the stand reading from various documents and answering an occasional question from Judge Charlene Gold. Her Honor was an unsympathetic woman with a long, gaunt face topped by a tangle of gray hair. She looked like a scrubbing brush. I didn't hold that against her. I probably looked like hell, too.

There were no reporters, as far as I could tell. Everyone who was there seemed to have an attorney on his or her arm. I guess this kind of hearing wasn't sexy enough.

Yet.

The whole thing was all over in less than a half-hour. None of the ostensibly wounded parties—Reynold Sterne or my Wiccan sisters—was present. Just the two sparring attorneys, both of whom spoke with passion about the rights to something that belonged to neither. It was surreal.

Before accepting the judge's offer to step down, I asked if I could say something for the record.

"You may," the judge said matter-of-factly, apparently expecting a plea for mutual love and understanding. I imagine she'd heard it all during her tenure on the bench.

But probably not this.

"Do you believe in ghosts, Your Honor?"

She and the attorneys all turned to me as one. No one in the gallery was talking or fidgeting.

"Are you serious?" she asked.

"I am, Your Honor."

"This is relevant *how*, Ms. Katz?" she asked.

I smiled thinly. "*I* don't believe in them, you see.

But I believe that someone is trying to make me *think* my house is haunted."

"Why would someone do that?" she asked.

"It could be to scare me into leaving." I looked directly at the open-mouthed Dickson. "Or it could be to convince me that I need constant spiritual protection." I glanced at the unflappable Bushyhead.

"I have a full calendar and the other pleaders will kindly forgive this discursion," Judge Gold sighed. "Will you explain and make it brief, Ms. Katz?"

"I will, Your Honor," I said. "I was awakened at two a.m. by noises in the den. I went downstairs and I saw someone in the shadows. When I went to call nine-one-one, the electricity was suddenly shut off. I hurried outside where I was rendered unconscious by an airborne toxin blown into my face by someone I didn't see."

"You were assaulted?" the judge asked.

"Ambushed and poisoned," I said. "The police and paramedics have a full report, and the doctor took a sample from my nasal passages. When I thought about it this morning, I realized that the tableau I saw downstairs was meant to resemble a Civil War encampment, I think—complete with a soldier in gray and sandbags."

"Your Honor!" Dickson protested.

"How do you know it wasn't a real manifestation?"

the leather-faced Joseph Bushyhead asked, turning from Dickson to the judge.

Which was exactly what I had hoped he would do. I didn't answer. Andrew A. Dickson did, however—which was exactly what I'd hoped *he* would do.

"Your Honor, lack of evidentiary support aside, this is irrelevant testimony," the attorney said. "If Ms. Katz experienced anything at all, it may have been a home invasion which she interrupted—"

"Or it may be a result of the opening of a door to the spirit world," Attorney Bushyhead countered.

"—*neither* of which should or can have any impact on a contract dispute," Attorney Dickson barreled on. "I would like to remind the court—I am *obligated* to remind the court that there are also at stake here the futures of many promising young scholars, who are devoting their theses to the work at hand."

"Your Honor, as we have been debating for the past thirty minutes, this is also a question of religious freedom," the Cherokee disagreed.

"Religious manipulation," Dickson countered. "The earlier agreement, prior to the hasty conversion of the site, should have priority."

Judge Gold asked for both men to be silent and looked at me. She seemed openly annoyed. "Ms. Katz, I have eaten at your deli. You make a good grilled cheese with turkey bacon and tomato."

"Thank you, Judge Gold."

"And you seem to be a thoughtful, hardworking, down-to-earth woman. However, in the matter before the court, we have not been impressed by your behavior to date. We are here because as Mr. Dickson has stated, the evidence suggests you were trying to overturn an already adjudicated matter by inviting the Wiccans into your home. I understand the shock of discovering what your uncle had agreed to, but your remedy makes me question your commitment to the legal process. You could have petitioned this court for a temporary restraining order. The road not taken is lined with billboards that advocate rational, proven tradition."

"I didn't drive a lot until I moved here, Your Honor," I said. "I'm still learning."

"At whose expense? Religion? Archaeological research? Your own health and well-being?"

There are times to defend one's self and there are times to shut up. I could hear my great-grandmother yelling in my ear, "*Sha! Sha!*" I did not speak.

"That said, I cannot tolerate the prehearing manipulation of a witness. Therefore, I'm going to order a recess until I can read the relevant reports of the police and medical personnel. This matter is adjourned until Monday morning at ten."

"Thank you, Your Honor," I said to a pair of dubious, deep-set eyes.

Dickson looked as if he wanted to protest but thought better of it. I had been watching their expressions carefully; both men seemed to have had no knowledge of what I had dropped on the courtroom. If one of their clients was responsible—and I was betting they were—these two were out of the loop.

The question, then, was who did it and why? And one thing more. There were now three poison victims: two fatal, one not, but all relatively back to back to back. That, plus my innate Jewish paranoia, would not let me shake the idea that in some way these events were all related.

Chapter 19

It was Saturday.

That was always a day for the tourist trade, and they dribbled in over the course of the day without anything approaching a "rush."

A visit from a police officer—not one of the two who had come to my home, but a Detective Olive Egan—confirmed that it was belladonna that was puffed in my *punim*. She said she would be going back to the house to search the grounds for evidence the other officers may have missed.

"May have?" I snorted. "They spent about five minutes looking around inside and out, and shared a flashlight."

"The focus of their investigation was not clear," she said evasively.

"You mean they thought the victim was the perp," I said.

"They made quick field judgments."

God, I hated cover-your-ass language. I gave up. Anyway, I shouldn't have bashed her for their incompetence. For all I knew, she was perfectly fine at her job. She showed me a satellite view of my home on an iPad, asked me to point out the spot where I was dusted, then asked me to try to describe my assailant. I told her I could not, it having been dark, me having been in a panic, and poison having clouded my vision. She thanked me, then cautioned me not to expect much since it had rained the night of the assault and whatever footprints or traces of powder might have been there were probably gone.

"Check for dead moles and chipmunks," I suggested.

This being Saturday, it meant that after brunch I was free to try and find out where the poison came from and who might've purchased it. While I knew that exotic herbs could be grown or mail-ordered, I also had a suspicion that this was not.

The health inspector's question about bamboo prompted me to look it up online. Easy to grow, innocuous . . . and chock-full of naturally occurring cyanide sugar. It would take a whole lot of garden space to grow that much bamboo.

Or a tiny bit of shelf space to keep it in powdered form. As at the local natural vitamin and herbalist emporium.

I was sure that Daniels and his crack little team had thought of this, too, but I also knew that the owner, Bill "Spud" Carla, was an unrepentant hippy who had lobbied hard at the state legislature for the struggling Safe Access to Medical Cannabis Act. I didn't know him, but I was willing to bet that he knew me.

His small, boxy shop was located on Oldham Street near Cowan. There was a security camera set up and blackened doors; you had to be video ID'd and buzzed in. I guess I was okay since the door hummed and clicked. I walked into the large, single room. It was lit with long fluorescent lights and looked like a tea shop, but it was musty with pungent odors I did not recognize. Spud was behind the counter. I knew that because he wore a lab coat that had his name embroidered in black. Standing a bony six-foot-five, with his bald head, thick eyeglasses, gray Fu Manchu moustache, and appropriately long fingernails, he looked like the last man on earth to whom you would entrust the passage of a bill or medical procedure. I know, one shouldn't judge by appearances. But this man had chosen to look weird. The least I could do was honor that.

When I entered, Spud was using a pair of those fingernails to remove pinches of some kind of leaves—they looked like bay leaves but I was sure they weren't—from a two-quart jar and place them on a small plastic scoop that sat on a digital scale. There was a brown paper bag beside it. He looked at me over the tops of his glasses.

"Good afternoon," he said with a low, raspy voice, the result, it sounded, of smoking regular cigarettes which I could smell on his clothes as I neared.

"Hi."

He looked back at his scale. "I'll be with you in ten blinks of a baby's eyes."

I didn't know how to respond to that except with a strained smile. I looked around the shop. There were shelves of vitamins along one wall, a large, wooden table in the center—it looked like one of those torture racks from which the wheel gizmos had been removed—and more of those big glass jars on the other walls. I recognized the names on seven of the dozens of containers I looked at. A small room beside the counter was labeled LIBRARY. I saw rows of books and DVDs with a female version of Spud at the counter: gray ponytail, no makeup, frumpy wardrobe.

"Now," he said apologetically, "what can I help you with today?"

"I'm not sure," I said. "My house was just consecrated as a Wiccan church and I felt I should familiarize myself with herbalism."

"You're Gwen Katz," he said.

I turned, still smiling my stiff smile. "That's right. How did you know? The smell of pastrami?"

"I would have smelled rotting meat on you as soon as you entered," he said. "Possibly before."

"That's quite a talent."

"Hardly. I am vegan." He said it with reverence, like a pacifistic extraterrestrial telling me his name. "It is a natural ability that has been buried by toxicity."

"I see. I guess I have a lot to learn."

"We all do," he said, "though purifying yourself would be a challenge because of your profession."

"Hey, it's not like I'm a lawyer or politician," I said.

His thin lips smiled a little at that. "Well said."

"But since you mention it, I was thinking—I've only been here a year. People have asked me for vegetarian dishes, and I've provided that. But I was thinking it might be fun to add some exotic spices, maybe make the salads a little healthier. Any suggestions? Like this jar," I said, tapping it lightly with a thumb knuckle. "Bamboo."

He walked slowly from behind the counter. "Why did you become a Wiccan?" he asked.

"What have you heard?" I asked back.

He grinned. "That you were looking to protect your home. Sally Biglake is a customer of good and long standing."

I felt a little uneasy now. Spud may have been skeletal, but he was an imposing figure. Especially trailing smoke and other disorienting smells like he'd just emerged from the Pit of Hell.

"I think she and I got off to an iffy start," I said. "She did me a big favor the other night and I was thinking, also, I might buy her a little gift."

He looked where my knuckle still rested. "Bamboo?"

"No, I was thinking about that for a Chinese dish I've been considering," I said.

"Probably not the best ingredient in that form," he said. "You may have noticed the label is red, not black."

"I did," I said, looking around. I had noticed but figured he just ran out of one kind of felt-tipped pen.

"It's poisonous in more than the smallest of small doses," he said.

"Then why sell it?"

He answered, "As poison. As an ingredient in all-natural pest control."

"Forgive me, but why would someone care about killing vermin naturally?"

"Because the ingredients return to the earth," he said. "A bird of prey might eat a dead rat. Metabolized bamboo would be less toxic to the predator than, say, lingering traces of indandione anticoagulants or 4-hydroxycoumarin found in over-the-counter rodenticides."

"Makes sense," I agreed.

He came closer. "Ms. Nash, please do not confuse veganism with being inherently naive or weak. The police asked about my bamboo and my rat poisons. I explained that, yes, an organically based compound would dissipate more rapidly and efficiently into the human body until only a very skilled forensic chemist would be able to correctly identify it. I suspect that quick discovery, not the latter, is the reason they surmised that one Tippi Montgomery died from ingesting the kind of mixture prepared in my shop. I emphasize 'the kind of.' Any competent herbalist could have prepared that mixture in their kitchen. And you will find, incidentally, that I do *not* sell mercury, which—according to the Herbal Defense Fund Association website—was the poison found in the body of the first victim, Ms. Montgomery's brother."

"True, but that was when someone, apparently, was trying to put the finger on my herring."

"It is quite right for you to defend your honor and that of your fish," he agreed. "None of which is my concern or my doing. I don't mean to sound callous, but I am constantly under suspicion and even assault from the authorities due to my activism. I am not responsible for the actions of my customers, only my own. And, like you, I look after the integrity of my product. Which brings me back to, what can I help you with today?"

One thing was certain: I'd been told.

"Sorry to have interrupted," I said with a nod toward the counter.

"You didn't. I finished that step."

I'd been told, again. I'd had enough of this. I'd learned that he sold what may have been used to kill Tippi Montgomery—but not definitively. I turned to go and saw, on the shelf, rows of his own remedies. They were packaged in little brown bags, like upscale tea leaves. Among them was one I'd seen before. It was called Karmamine and had a picture of a wave.

"What's this for?" I asked.

He was still standing where I'd left him. "Sea-sickness," he replied.

Great, I thought. So maybe Yutu shopped here, too. Maybe he had a reason for killing Lippy. Or Barron again—he could have purchased the Karmamine and, by the way, let's have some all natural rat poison for the boat. Mad had had access to Lippy's food. I didn't know who had access to Tippi. And what did any of that have to do with the trumpet case going missing, then turning up—if anything?

Was everyone in my circle a potential suspect? Was everyone involved? Should I just go home, remove myself from events, and let them take their own course? What was it my great-grandmother used to say about why she never read a newspaper? *Let the world knock its own heads together.*

I left knowing little more than I had before, only glad that I was out of that rank tomb with its walking cadaver.

I headed back across the Cumberland River with almost nothing in my head. Or, rather, nothing particularly motivational. Dammit, I needed a hobby that didn't involve dead bodies. I was thinking about where to go. I didn't want to go to the

house, where the Wiccan tent was still pitched; I
hadn't seen Sally that morning and I suspected she
wasn't there since her cat was sitting outside the
flap, the familiar waiting. I didn't want to go to
the deli which I never seemed to escape. What
about a movie? A museum? Something different,
like a hot air balloon ride? A hike? There was the
Leatherwood Ford Trail that went to the Angel
Falls Overlook. That sounded—sweaty.

"How about you just keep driving and head
north, to New York?"

And then I put something else in my brain.
Before going to bed the night before, I had
downloaded the song Luke and Mad had been
humming—"More Coffee." I turned on my iPod,
gave it a few listens. It was as catchy as everyone
had said, with the added benefit that the electric
harp was soothing in a kind of full-body-harmonic-
New-Age way. It was like "Achy Breaky Heart" and
"Livin' La Vida Loca" except that you didn't hate
yourself for liking it.

I didn't go home or to the deli. It was a very
clear and warmish day so I went to the Bicenten-
nial Capitol Mall State Park and walked around a
bit. The nineteen-acre park, one of the great
urban open spaces in the nation, had been newly
restored after disastrous 2010 flooding. I hadn't
been here before but the fountains and columns
of the fix-up were stunning. I walked from the
capitol building through the Court of Three Stars

with its stately ninety-five-bell carillons. I strolled by the Tennessee River Wall and the thirty-one geyserlike fountains representing the state's rivers and waterways. Then I picked up a pulled-pork wrap and Coke at the farmer's market—take that, vegan-alien!—and plopped myself on the grass. I had a flashback to Central Park in the early fall, when it was still warm and the trees were only just beginning to turn and there were distant sounds of traffic and kids with balls and Frisbees and dogs, just like now. I thought about what had filled my head then, the short-term worries and ambitions. I actually missed them. They were manageable bites. Finish analyzing this portfolio. Get my hair done for that date. Make sure to pick up Mom's birthday cake. Pick up a couple of magazines so I won't go crazy staying home on Yom Kippur.

Who was *that girl and where did she go?* I wondered. *When* did she go? It wasn't a precise time and place and I couldn't even trace the process. All I knew is that she seemed like someone else. What I couldn't figure out was whether I was wiser now or simply beaten down and jaded. I did know that I was more *hamisch* now—down-to-earth, a real person.

"They were both you," I murmured. "Only now I'm the tree without the trimmings."

The phalanxes of bells rang the hour. That was a signal to come back to the present. I did. Sitting here, doing nothing at all, life didn't seem so bad.

I was earning enough money, I was my own boss, and—okay—there was some *tsuris* with the house. And the "fella" situation could be better. But lots of people had those problems and worse. Like the fact that "More Coffee" was still playing in my head even though the iPod was in the car.

I checked e-mails—there were zero—so rather than feel like a loser and put my phone away, I looked up the gal who performed the song.

Ximene Gonzalez Gallego, born 1989, a winner on the Spanish talent TV show *Operación Éxito* in 2009, released an album that same year which was a moderate hit, another album in 2011 which got some attention here, and then wham— *"Más café."* Romantically linked to Flamenco guitarist Juanito Mantilla, to Basque singer Nino Laboa, to fiery young Berliner Philharmoniker conductor Kurt Furtwangler, and presently—

Oh ho.

I stopped. That was interesting. She was currently dating Chimanga Strong, the president of the Southern Free International Bank. According to the entry, Strong was also the founder and financier behind Cotton Saint Tunes.

"So Fly Saucer has a bankro daddy," I muttered. That in itself wasn't so strange as the fact that

Fly Saucer didn't seem to make a big deal out of having a big record. I wondered if even Luke knew that it was his. Maybe it happened so often for Fly it wasn't anything special.

Dammit.

There was only one person who would be able to help unravel whatever had happened, and that was the cop who was already trying to figure the whole thing out.

"Don't even think about that," I told myself. "The day is too sweet for compromise."

Though I did wonder—because I'm like a dog with a bone; I can't leave things be, even when they're bad for me—what would I do if he happened to walk by? Coincidences like that did occur. Would I want him to sit with me as just someone I know or the cop on the case—or would I want him to walk on? If I could pick and choose how he was going to integrate with my life, he could sit down. If not, he could stroll on by. Not that I expected him to stop. He had to have seen the police report about the assault outside my house. He hadn't even texted to see how I was.

I ate my delightfully greasy wrap and dripped some kind of barbecue sauce on the grass. I sat on my suddenly unmotivated *tuchas*. I smiled at the cute park ranger who ambled by. He looked impassively back at me, which made me feel old and ugly and I suddenly hated him and whatever bimbo belle he was dating. I tried to change the mental subject and think about where I wanted to be a year from now.

Yes, things are okay. But I knew that I did not want to be back in this park next fall, by myself, wondering where I wanted to be a year from then . . .

Chapter 20

I had a little bit of an epiphany while I was lying in the park.

I was thinking about my mother and how much she would have liked the trees and the occasional twittering birds. She was always too busy and too concerned about me to worry about herself. I realized that my life down here was pure Mom. I worked, I looked after my staff, I did my little part in these various homicide investigations, all so I wouldn't have to do what I'd just done: reflect on my own life. Not that there was anything wrong with helping others. But if you put yourself on the sidelines, pretty soon there was no time left to do anything about your own life.

I honestly didn't know how to change that. I didn't know if I *could* change it. I remember my mother saying how *her* mother was always taking on too much, especially things that were none of her business. Maybe it was in my DNA. But I decided, then, to try and give myself perspective instead of being swept along with the current. I'd keep a journal, and resolved to write down something new I'd learned every day—even if it was something small, like, "Mature shade trees actually have a personality" or "pulled pork causes acid reflux and makes me *grepts*." One way or the other, the same time next year would be different.

It was late afternoon when I finally picked myself up and took a walk through the city. It was early evening when I found myself on 3rd Avenue not far from Union Street. I decided to go over to The Oatmeal Stallion. I'd never been and I decided I wanted to see a place where Lippy had played. I wondered if the police even knew about the connection. Fly had said he'd screwed up here. I wondered how.

It was still early so there was no bruiser at the red velvet ropes, no one behind the black velvet ropes that marked the smoking area, and no problem getting in. Things didn't really heat up in this part of town until the hours moved back into single digits.

The bar was a horseshoe with tables packed tightly on both sides. A floor for the jazz band was at the open part of the horseshoe. There were two small dance areas on either side of that. Even though the club was open, it felt closed. There were only a few customers—mostly tourists, it looked like—and the bartender was busier with his cell phone than he was preparing drinks. I don't drink much, but when I do, I order something fruity like an apricot sour. It didn't really taste like liquor, but just one made me very nominally, pleasantly light-headed.

I sat away from the door, near the stage. It was tomb quiet, surprisingly depressing. But it did enable me to hear some yelling from somewhere behind the stage.

"Trouble with the talent?" I asked the bartender.

"Nah, it's the big boss," said the young man, who had a treble and base clef cut in either side of his scalp. He said it without looking up from his text. "He likes to yell."

"You mean, Fly? He seems so laid back."

The kid snickered. "Not the Fly man. The *big* boss. Mr. S."

"Oh. Is Ximene with him?" I joked.

The kid snickered. "She's on tour in Asia."

"Maybe that's why the big boss is so cross," I said. "Hey, can I ask you a question?" I didn't want for him to answer. "Did you know Lippy Montgomery?"

He looked up for the first time. "Why? You CSI?"

"Nope. Just a friend who misses him, wanted to talk about him."

"I didn't really know him," he said, and went back to texting.

"But you know he was killed."

"DYD, I got that tweet," he told me—or rather,

told me off—then shambled away. Least sociable bartender ever; the kid didn't seem interested in conversation—at least, not with an old lady. And, by the way, after puzzling over it for a while, it wasn't until the next day, when I asked Luke, that I learned DYD meant "Drink Your Drink" with an implied ALMA—"And Leave Me Alone."

The muffled shouting rose and fell, like the sounds of a trumpet with a wah-wah mute. After a few minutes, a man I assumed to be Chimanga Strong emerged. He wore a tailored gray suit that probably cost more than my car and he trailed Clive Christian No. 1, which costs about two grand a bottle. I recognized it from an insert in a women's magazine. It was something you were supposed to treat your man to—which, even if I had one, I never would.

He didn't look like a man who, on paper at least, had it all.

What surprised me was who followed him out. It was Grant.

He was in his off-duty clothes—jeans, a button-down white shirt, blue blazer—and was poking at his cell phone, looking down. He was nearly past me when he happened to look up. He was facing ahead. I was on his right as he passed. He saw me peripherally and turned, like a rubbernecker at a traffic accident. He kept moving forward a moment longer, then stopped. Once they found me, his eyes never left me. He hesitated, then took a few steps toward me. His look was a strange mix of incredulous, glad, and hostile.

"Hey," I said. I felt pretty neutral, maybe a little guarded; that was the least provocative word I could think of.

He looked around. First at the adjoining seats and bar, then at the room. "You here alone?"

"I was," I said. That was the apricot sour answering. My brain didn't want to extend the invite. Or did it? I was confused.

He dipped his forehead toward the stool beside me. "May I?"

"Only if you promise not to buy me a drink," I said. "One's my limit."

"I know," he said.

There it was—a trace of bitterness. Hopefully, he got it out of his system. Otherwise, this was going to be a very short reunion.

"You okay?" he asked. "I saw the police report."

Before I could answer, the bartender wandered over. He was no longer texting, seemed ready to do his job. Grant ordered a light beer.

"I'm all right," I said. My ears heard my voice and I didn't like how glum I sounded. I cleared my throat. "I spoke to a detective after the NPD decided I hadn't imagined the whole thing."

"I heard. Detective Egan's very thorough—she even asked where I was that night."

"Sorry."

"No need. I told her I was at the movies."

I didn't press. I didn't care if he went alone, with a fellow officer, or with Miss Tennessee.

"Anyway, Detective Egan scraped the boiler-room floor," he went on. "Concrete is pretty absorptive and she said that room is hot. She's convinced they'll find some DNA. That'll rule me out."

"Will it rule anyone *in*?"

"Not really," he admitted. "It's good to have, see if it matches anyone on file. But you can't subpoena samples without probable cause."

God bless the ACLU, I thought insincerely. I was all for due process, but not for laws that protected the perps at the expense of the victims.

"So," I said, "what are you doing here? If I may ask."

"Following up on some forensics of my own," he said with uncustomary reserve.

"Officially, but not," I said, looking his wardrobe up and down.

"Yeah. Some people—you don't want to come at them head-on."

"Or they lawyer up."

Grant just smiled a little as his beer arrived. I thought hard, pushing past the thin scrim of the drink. Something he found in the trumpet case brought him here. What and why? It had to be something too small for me to have noticed. I glanced at the bartender. Hair? Cigarette ash from outside?

A spilled drink in some crusted-over corner of velvet, maybe one of the house specialties?

"So what do you make of your home invader?" Grant asked. "Something Sally worked up?"

"To become my savior?" I shrugged. "I suppose she could have rigged a door or window when she was inside. And she shops where they sell belladonna."

"At that nutjob Spud's place?" he laughed. "He's got the drill down pat."

"What do you mean?"

"We think he grows and stores his 'misdemeanor drugs' in a van. He knows what a team with a search warrant looks like and he moves the van to a spot off-property, where it can't be searched."

"Can't you just get two search warrants? One for the building and one for the van?"

"We tried that," Grant said. "Joint NPD and FBI investigation two years ago. He figured that out, too, from the jackets. He had his girlfriend spray the interior of the van with Agent White."

"Who is that, a mole?"

Grant nearly spit a mouthful of beer. "Good one."

"What was?"

He stared at me. "Agent White. You made it a person."

I looked back at him, totally confused. "Isn't it?"

"You're serious," he said. "No, Agent White is a powerful defoliant, one of the 'rainbow herbicides' used by our armed forces until the mid-1980s. It's a deadlier form of Agent Orange. Spud got his hands on a drum of the stuff and keeps it to kill the pot. Legally, a dead plant is not evidence of intent to sell, which is the real crime. Just getting into the vehicle to get it out would have required HAZMAT equipment—PD and Bureau rules—which enters into a new area of legal wrangling. We would have to declare a state of emergency, close down several blocks of the city, put choppers in the air in case the suspect attempts to flee . . . just not worth it for a few pot plants."

"Or belladonna or bamboo cyanide," I said.

He was still looking at me. "You've been doing your homework."

"I've been scrubbing my name clean. Again."

He turned to his beer. "Your name was never really in danger. Not for that."

There was bitter dig number two. The apricot sour gave him a pass. I looked at the dark wood of the bar. The lights were a hazy smear, reflecting my thoughts.

Grant took pity on me. "The officers didn't find any indication of forced entry at your place. Did anyone—"

"I'm sorry," I blurted. "I truly am. I circled the wagons. I don't know why. Well, actually, I do—but they were my wagons, my cowboys, and also my Indians."

"Look, I was a little over-eager, I know that. I

didn't allow for the fact that maybe I'm not what you want."

I snickered. "How many drinks did you see me take in the months we dated?"

"One. It was sherry."

"Right. Do you think I'd be sitting here by myself if I knew what I wanted? Half of me wants to run back home—I mean home-home, New York—and the other half of me wants to take on every challenge that's facing me here."

Grant swallowed more beer. "I wish you the best of luck with that," he said. "I do. Because some of what you think are challenges are—*were*—allies who happened to be in the line of fire."

I hate it when pronouns are used to discuss proper nouns whose identities are perfectly well-known. I finished my drink and put a twenty on the counter. I wanted to say, "Some allies are like Lichtenstein—neutral and dull." But I didn't. I wanted to leave things somewhat sociable.

"I should be going," I said. "I have a couple of messes to deal with."

"Two questions before you go?" Grant said-asked.

I turned to him with a wary "go ahead" look on my face. I had no idea what subject he was about to broach.

"Did you pick at the lining inside Lippy's case?" he asked.

I wasn't happy with that, but it was better than a question about "us." I asked him why he asked.

"Because we found slight scrape marks, like a knife or letter opener would make."

"Did you?" I asked. Which was as good as a confession.

"Tampering with evidence is a felony," he said. "But let's pretend we're not concerned with silly details. Did you find anything there?"

"I'll answer that if you tell me what you found that brought you here," I said.

He considered the offer. "A strand of facial hair."

"Strong is clean shaven."

"A lot of the musicians here aren't," Grant said. "He's not happy about a criminal investigation that could have blowback on him. Your turn. What did *you* find?"

"Ink," I replied. "A couple of lowercase letters might have been—a 'p' and a 'p' at least that is what I thought it looked like. I'm sure you saw them, too."

"That's all?" he pressed. "No letter that went along with that?"

"I would've told you if I had," I said. "I want you to find whoever killed Lippy and Tippi."

"Was there any reason in particular you looked there?" Grant asked.

"Tippi had mentioned that her brother had some kind of treasure. I thought she meant a map and that it was something he may have mentioned to Robert Barron. Y'know? A map from Hawaii, something leading to a sunken galleon, an old piece of paper tucked in the case he bought there."

"Worth killing for?" Grant asked.

"I don't know," I admitted. "I have no perspective on what motivates anyone. I mean, Wall Street gets dumped on, but who isn't greedy? Is a buried campsite worth more than a person's home? Is a *farkakt* religion that put down roots in my boiler room more important than bona fide historical research? Is a bad boy more appealing to me than a good boy? Like I said before, I have no answers."

That last one was for him, and he knew it. He finished his beer.

"You had a second question?" I said. "Or was it buried in the others."

"You cut me off earlier," he said, slipping from the stool and paying for his beer.

"Apologies."

He dismissed it with a little shake of his head. "I was going to ask—since there apparently wasn't a break-in—if anyone besides you had a key to your home?"

"Just my dear, dear friend Dr. Reynold Sterne," I said. "At least, that's what K-Two told me."

"Sterne is the professor in charge of the dig?"

"Yeah."

"Is he really your dear friend?" Grant asked. The

question was in earnest and slightly wounded. It was almost sweet.

"I can't stand the *shmuck*," I assured him.

Grant relaxed into a smile. "Well, you might want to find out where that key was. Or I can, if you'd like."

"Thanks, but I'll let Detective Egan do it," I said.

Grant's expression shifted from neutral to mildly distressed. It reflected the frustration he obviously felt at his lack of progress in recovering lost territory. "Just trying to help," he said weakly.

"I know. And I appreciate it."

"Right. Great."

He forced a smile and left. I moved slowly to give him time to get away. I wanted to be alone when I went back to my car. This relationship was like a yo-yo that kept hitting me in the chin each time I pulled it up. If it couldn't be the way he wanted, then it couldn't be. I'd already had one of those. I didn't want another.

Chapter 21

The Wiccans convened that night at around eight and decided that a prayer meeting, with chanting, was a good idea.

There were about a dozen of them. I watched through my living-room window as they arrived in a van—except for Sally, who came on her bike. I didn't know anyone other than her and Mad; I certainly didn't know there were that many witches in Nashville. Or maybe they'd been bussed in to make the case that my property was a working temple. I also noticed a sedan with smoky-black windows parked across the street, in front of a house that had been foreclosed about six months ago. My guess—based on nothing but mistrust—is that it was Attorney Andrew A. Dickson III, recording the comings and goings of Wiccans.

I wasn't worried about any noise the Wiccans might make. Given the amount of chainsawing and motor overhauling my neighbors did at all hours, they weren't likely to call the cops on some pagan dissonance.

I was tired from my little adventure—and the stressful week—and later as I lay in bed, half drowsing, I heard the nonmelodic, minor-key *dovening* that drifted into the room.

No, that's not right, I thought. *It's more like* kvetching; *a bunch of women whining.* The difference was a kind of tension that came from the back of the throat. You grow up in a home like mine, you become aware of how women complain.

Lying in bed, my eyes shut, I hovered between sleep and wakefulness as the chant hung faintly in the air around me, like a mosquito net. I thought about how much I had enjoyed the day and how I needed more of those and how much I didn't want to go back to the deli. When I wasn't walking the floor or cutting things up in the kitchen, I was stuck in an office that was stuck in the past— except when I was examining the trumpet case, I smiled. That was fun, that was different. It was a challenge. It had a purpose. It—

Wait a minute.

My eyes opened and I looked at the dark ceiling. I was surprised that I had remembered a word from high school geometry. It was pretty impressive what the mind could do when it wasn't focused on a subject. Like thinking about the trumpet case.

Why didn't I see that before?

Because you're an accountant-turned-deli-manager, not a musicologist, I told myself.

I wondered if Grant had picked it up. I turned on the light beside my bed, switched on my charging cell phone, and sent a text to Raylene. She probably wasn't asleep yet and, sure enough, she wrote back in less than a minute. Just two words:

I'll check.

Perfect.

I turned off the light, lay back, and hoped I could sleep. I did, easily and deeply. My subconscious had done its job and was as eager for rest as the remainder of my brain.

I was full of enthusiasm the next morning because there was a sense of proactivity and discovery in my soul. I was looking forward to something with a different set of challenges.

Raylene arrived with what I'd asked for—one of the business cards Fly had given her, with his personal phone number written in gold Sharpie on the back.

"Are you expecting him not to be here?" she asked as we did the morning prep, checking napkin holders and filling the ketchup and mustard jars.

"That's always a possibility," I allowed.

"So what's up? Are you thinkin' of *dating* him? Because if you are, I'd say you haven't got enough of what he wants."

"What would that be?"

"*Tookas*," she said, slapping her own rump.

"It's *tuchas*," I said with a guttural *ch*, "and isn't that a little stereotypical?"

"Call it what you want, I see him checkin' *me* out when I walk away." Raylene pointed to the mirror above the counter. "He likes my *toochas*."

"Well, don't worry about mine," I said.

"Will the two of you please change the topic?" Thom asked from behind the counter. She seemed mildly but sincerely offended.

"Hey, *butt* out, Thom!" Luke shouted from the back.

It was definitely time to get to work.

We didn't open until ten on Sunday mornings. It was our lightest day, a drizzle of tourists from opening until we closed at six. It was typically just a break-even day but I stayed open because it gave everyone an extra shift.

I wasn't willing to go so far as to say it was Fly Saucer's facial hair the police lab had found in the trumpet case and that he'd gone into hiding—that wouldn't have done him much good—but I was willing to bet that Chimanga Strong got him on the phone the night before to ask him if it might be. And if so, why. Which meant that Fly had probably spent the morning talking to an attorney. It was sad that even if someone were innocent, it was necessary to hire a lawyer.

As soon as we had a break around ten-thirty, I called the number on Raylene's card.

I was weighing whether or not to ask about "the fuzz" if he picked up. He didn't, but someone did—just after four rings, when I was pretty sure I was headed for voice mail.

"This is Mr. Saucer's line."

I recognized that voice but I couldn't place it. "This is Gwen Katz. Is Mr. Saucer available? I want to dish with the Saucer." It just came out; I couldn't resist and I didn't apologize to whoever I was talking with. Anxiety sometimes makes me punny.

"Ms. Katz, Mr. Saucer is not available."

"Who is this?" I asked.

"Attorney Dickson," he replied smoothly. "Is there a message for Mr. Saucer?"

"Yes," I said. "He—forgot something the last time he was here. Just tell him I'll give it to him next time I see him."

"May I tell him what it is?"

"No."

I hung up. Hard. I could have respected him if he were an advocate for the downtrodden, but he smelled like an opportunist. When it suited him, he helped them. When it didn't, as with Thom's brother, he helped boot them from their businesses. Wall Streeters got a bad rap, but at least we were consistent: it was all about the money. Virtually every lawyer I ever knew did not have that same kind of compass. Maybe because most of them were future politicians at heart interested in the corridors of power.

Sunday dragged. It was livened only by an early afternoon visit from a very, very angry Robert Barron. He literally exploded through the door like Uther Pendragon pouncing on the Lady Igraine. Only King Arthur would not be the issue from this union.

He stood by the cash register as his eyes sought me out. They found me behind the counter, making coffee.

"You did this!" he yelled as he walked over.

The six customers stopped what they were doing and looked over.

"Good afternoon, Robert," I said calmly, having no idea what I'd done. I was pretty sure he hadn't been drinking, though; his eyes were clear and his walk was steady, purposeful. "You want to turn the volume down?"

"I'll turn nothing down except my *bed sheets*!" he roared.

That didn't even make sense, but then all a guy

like him needed was a loud voice—which he was using now.

"You had sex with Yutu and now he doesn't want to have anything to do with me!"

Raylene and Luke gawked at me with amused, perverse interest.

"You had a threesome?" Raylene muttered.

"No, with just Yutu," I said.

This wasn't the time to get into *shtick.* Thom looked as if she'd seen Medusa. Two of the three couples in the dining room asked for their food "to go." The third couple—bus driver Jackie and her gal-pal Leigh—looked on with rapt fascination.

"I don't know what you said to him," Barron said through his teeth, "but Yutu got home and called the whole expedition off!"

"I think it was seeing *you* naked that scared him," I said. "He got to see you for what you really are—a hustler."

Barron stalked closer. I had my hand on the glass coffeepot in case I needed to defend myself. There were many ways in which hot coffee could sober a man.

"You and your opinions, your judgments," he snarled as he reached the counter. "You people—always so suspicious!"

"You mean women?" I asked. "Or accountants? Or restaurateurs—?"

"I mean *you people,*" he said. "You stick to your

own, you don't trust anyone outside the group. Now I've got that problem with the damn Eskimos, too. That kind of anti-Americanism makes me sick."

"Is *that* what it is?" I said. "Because I'm an American—so is Thom, so are Leigh and Jackie, so is everyone here!"

"Then how come I'm the outsider?"

"Because you're a bully?" I said. "As for 'we people,' it's true—we've found that it's safer *not* to get on the train just because someone tells you to. If that makes you 'sick,' then *hindert hayzer zol er hobn, in yeder hoyz a hindert tsimern, in yeder tsimer tsvonsik betn un kadukhes zol im varfn fin eyn bet in der tsveyter.*"

That stopped him dead. It also confused the hell out of Raylene, Luke, Thom, and the two lesbian lovers.

"It was my great-grandmother's favorite Yiddish expression," I said. "'A hundred houses shall he have, in every house a hundred rooms, and in every room twenty beds, and a delirious fever should drive him from bed to bed.'"

The ensuing silence was broken when Raylene said, "Girl, that's nasty!"

Barron did not know quite how to respond. His mouth contorted as if it wanted to say things, but he decided against it. He just shook his head angrily. "I won't be coming *here* again," he said at last.

"There goes our diversity award," I replied. "We've got everything but an unrepentant redneck."

Jackie and Leigh applauded lightly. I heard Luke say an approving, "Duuuude!" behind me. Raylene was leaning on a chair, ready to swing it. Thom was still frozen.

But Barron had been unmanned. He left angrier than he'd arrived. I would have to find out who made the glass in our front door so I could post something online: it withstood a ferocious exit.

There was a moment of silence and then an audible exhale followed by more reserved applause from the two remaining customers. I had a kind of fluttering anxiety attack in my knees that ran up to my waist, but I was behind the counter so I was able to lean the front of my thighs against it. I carefully put the coffeepot back in its place.

"Duuude," Luke repeated.

That pretty much said it all.

We got back to work as new customers arrived, though I did not escape a wave-over from Leigh. I walked over and sat down—my still-wobbly legs demanded it.

"That was a thing of beauty," Leigh said, still aglow. "You stood up for everyone, girl. All of us so-called minorities."

"It just happened that way," I assured her.

"Maybe, but if we all stood shoulder-to-shoulder

against bullies, they would be exposed as blowhards, like you did with that a-hole."

"It could just as easily have gone another way," I said. "He could have had a gun."

"Those are the risks of defending our liberties," Jackie said.

"I have a thing about men telling me what to do," I smiled. "And referring to me as 'you people' as if any group is homogeneous."

"Hey, watch your language." Leigh grinned.

I didn't get it. She had to explain that I'd said "homo."

I returned her smile. I was more anxious now than I had been before.

"Hey, you want to have a girls' night?" Jackie asked. "Nothing like what you apparently had the other night—"

"Unless you want to." Leigh winked.

"I was just thinking maybe you could use the distraction," Jackie went on.

"Yeah, and we could show you one of Tippi's movies."

That knocked the "dis" off my "interested."

"You have the one with Lippy in it?"

"We do own that," Leigh said.

"I accept," I said impulsively. "Just to watch. The movie, I mean."

"We are happy to share with you," Leigh replied.

Jackie gave me the address and I told them I'd be there around a little after six. I said I'd bring the sandwiches. And I knew, already, what I would learn that day: whether going home with a pair of women who happened to be gay and who understood and supported me, to watch porn, was a good idea—or a great one.

Chapter 22

Jackie and Leigh lived in a one bedroom apartment on the top floor of a new faux stone building called—I'm not kidding—the Cuirass. The three-story building was decorated with sculptures of ancient armor on the exterior and interior walls and was located on Edmondson Pike, halfway between Sevenmile Park and William Whitfield Park.

The couple had made the most of their limited resources by incorporating beer cans and hubcaps into the design of furniture and various fixtures like lamps and picture frames. Inside those frames were pictures of the ladies with what looked like parents, nieces, and nephews. I'll admit I felt a twinge of—not jealousy, but wistfulness. Not only didn't I have any close family left, I didn't have close family even when they'd been nearby. I had no framed photos of my parents at the house.

What photos I had were stuffed in a USPS priority mail pouch, which was in a box in a closet in the den.

So I wasn't sentimental. Maybe that was a problem, too.

The ladies had changed from jeans and button-down shirts into sweat clothes. They hadn't dressed up, which was nice, since I hadn't bothered to go home to change. This wasn't a date, after all.

I handed the bag with the sandwiches and sides to Leigh, who asked me what I wanted to drink. I had brought Diet 7-Up and asked for that, on ice. They didn't try to push wine or beer on me and I appreciated that. It was difficult to process the fact that I was with nonjudgmental people. I helped them set things up on the table, which looked like it was made from a car lift with butcher block laid across the top.

We chatted a little, something we didn't do much of at the deli, and I was surprised to learn that they'd been together, openly, since high school back in the early 1990s. That took some courage.

"You want to eat while we watch?" Leigh asked, after hearing my sad story.

I said it was up to them. They said they preferred it.

"Otherwise, you have to pay attention to the story, which isn't much, or make fun of it, which one of us doesn't appreciate—"

"Me," Jackie raised her hand. "If you're watching a movie, you should *watch* it."

"—or else you have to keep yourself busy some other way," Leigh said, with a little smile that didn't bother me. It didn't bother me, not because it lacked a sexual component, but because it didn't come with the kind of pressure I always feel from men.

So we ate with the plates on cloth napkins spread on our laps. Leigh sat between Jackie and me.

Come Blow Your Horny was my first-ever hi-def porn experience. Not that I had a lot of porn-watching under my belt, so to speak. It looked nothing like any jazz club I'd ever seen; it was mostly white and red velvet drapes where walls should have been. Small blue spotlights added a harshness to the fabric and smoke formed a tester above the set—more than could have been produced by anyone smoking. The costumes looked like they came from thrift shops or someone's trunk in the attic, which they probably did.

Lippy was in the very first scene, tooting "Boogie Woogie Bugle Boy" in the background. It was the liveliest thing on the screen as everyone else said "Hi" and "Are you here alone?" and poor Tippi moved through them all asking, "Candy? Cigarettes?"

Sex happened—all kinds—before Lippy was

back playing trumpet. We had finished our dinner by then, which was fortunate; otherwise I would have spit it out, hard.

"Holy crap," I said as I turned an ear toward the flat screen. I ignored the fact that Leigh's and Jackie's hands were roaming Leigh's and Jackie's bodies.

"What?" Leigh asked, startled.

"Can you rewind or scroll back or whatever you do with this?"

"Sure." Leigh grabbed the remote from the coffee table, a tailgate resting on wooden crates. "How far?"

"To when Lippy appeared in this scene. And crank up the volume, please."

The image jerked backward. Leigh stopped it just as Tippi—after a lengthy, claustrophobic interlude in a cab, which I guessed was cheaper to hire than a limo—walked back into the club. It was only the second time in about twenty minutes that she had her clothes on, a little French maid number. It broke my heart to see her alive and seemingly comfortable. Fortunately, I had something else to think about when Leigh released the button and the image began to play. I listened carefully.

"What is it?" Jackie asked.

"I think it's the treasure," I said. "What do you hear?"

"Lippy and background noise—which includes

someone's cell phone ringing before they were invented."

"The song," I said impatiently.

The women listened silently.

"You're right," Leigh said. "I do know that." She started humming along. "That sounds a lot like 'More Coffee.'"

"So?" Jackie asked.

"So how old is this movie?" I asked. "Four, five years? That song is about two months old."

The women were silent for a moment and then Leigh scrolled back, listened again. "You know, even though they're very similar, they're not exact."

"That's true," I agreed.

"Seems to me Lippy would have had a tough time proving that a melody in an obscure porn film was ripped off."

"That's true, too," I said. "Still, Lippy told his sister he was onto some kind of treasure. He didn't tell her what. Maybe this was it? Maybe he was bargaining with the thief for a cut. Maybe the thief didn't want to pay it . . . or maybe he or she didn't want to be exposed. That kind of theft could be a career ender."

"So they killed him instead?" Leigh said dubiously. "Premeditated with poison?"

"That kind of thing could sink a company," I said.

Jackie shook her head. "Even if the song was

ripped off, you said Tippi didn't know what the treasure was. Why kill her?"

"Yeah, that's a big hole in the theory," I admitted.

The two women sat there, quite still; whatever mood had been building, I'd killed it deader than a salami. I felt bad about that. I had never really had sexual power over anyone or any situation. It figured I'd have it where it did me absolutely no good.

"You want another beverage?" Jackie asked after a time.

"No thanks."

Jackie got up to get refills for herself and Leigh. Leigh popped the DVD from the player, put it in a plastic sleeve, and handed it to me. She shut off the TV; clearly, we weren't going back to the porn flick. I thanked her for the movie and took out my cell phone to Google the song.

"That's interesting," I said.

"What is?" Leigh asked.

"It says 'More Coffee' was written by De F Chicken."

Jackie returned with two bottles of beer and another can of 7-Up. "Maybe a pseudonym for a group—like a jam session?"

"Or it could be some kind of joke," Leigh said.

I thought for a moment. "'F Chicken' has to be Funky Chicken, but hip-hop-ified—'def' Chicken."

"As in 'Do the Funky Chicken'?" Leigh asked, demonstrating her herky-jerky moves.

I nodded charitably.

"Why would anybody come up with an obviously phony name like that one?" Jackie asked.

"To throw the real composer off the scent," I suggested.

Jackie was shaking her head again. "I still think the odds are pretty 'out there' that someone would have seen this nothing little flick, heard a couple of bars of a song playing in the background—when what they came to see is in the foreground—and decided that it would make a great hit to launch an international singing career."

I had to agree that she made more sense than I did.

Until, thinking about a connection between the song and Lippy, I went back to the trumpet case—

"What if that wasn't where the person heard it?" I said. I still had my cell phone out and looked at my photos. I found the picture I had taken of the back side of the paste. I showed it to the ladies. "What do you make of this?"

"A 'pp,'" Leigh said.

"Or an upside-down 'bb,'" Jackie remarked.

Leigh hunched closer to me. "It could be a mirror image of letters, like 'dd.'"

"But it's not!" I said suddenly, with a "eureka" all but preceding the statement. "What if they're musical notes? Or an indication—what the hell is it?"

I thought back to my ill-fated piano lessons. "What did 'pp' stand for—very soft?"

The women looked from the phone to me. They clearly didn't know. It didn't matter. It meant something in music.

"The treasure," I said. "Lippy must have written the song down at some point. Maybe he'd worked on it for years. I'm guessing he knew he had a good, catchy tune and was busy *patschkieing* with it on his street corner."

"He was what?" Leigh asked.

"Just horsing around with it, riffing. Someone heard it. Someone knew he had a written copy stuffed in a loose flap in the case. Someone decided they needed to get that copy."

"That's a lot of conjecture, still," Leigh said.

"It is, but that record came out on Fly Saucer's label—and both he and Lippy were in the deli at the time he was poisoned."

Leigh whistled. "That's a big accusation, girl."

"I'm not making one, yet—only saying it's a possibility."

"Maybe you can tell the police informally," Jackie suggested. "Are you still friendly with that detective?"

"I wouldn't put it quite that way."

"But you can still tell him what you think?" Jackie asked.

Actually, I never could, I thought. "I don't know.

I'm going to sleep on this. Let's keep this between us, okay?"

"Of course," Jackie said.

"I don't suppose you want to see another movie," Leigh said.

"I think I'm done for the day. But this was really helpful, and you two were great. Nice place and perfect hosts."

We agreed to do a less abbreviated girls' movie night when things were a little calmer. The seductive undercurrent aside, they were nice ladies and I enjoyed hanging with them. In fact, I relished the change.

But I had other things on my mind as I left, such as how I was going to get to Fly Saucer without going through Grant or Andrew Dickson III or any of the other men who were always getting in my way. Because, for want of anything more pressing, that independence was suddenly very, very important.

Chapter 23

I drove home in a muddle.

On the one hand, I was suddenly energized. On the other, I had nowhere to put it. Going to Fly Saucer's home—even assuming I could get the address, which wasn't on the card Raylene had given me—was not an option.

Or was it?

Fly had obviously been with Dickson when he saw who was calling and handed over the phone. What if I sent him something he couldn't pass over and couldn't ignore?

I thought about it on the way home—then decided to go to the deli instead. I didn't want to be where the Wiccans could spy on me. About the only ones I trusted in my life—*with* my life—were my staff and the two gal-pals.

Because it was Sunday evening, I had no trouble

parking out front. I went in, locked the door behind me, and kept the lights off until I went to my office. I shut the door and sat with my cell phone in front of me. I felt like I did when I was a kid and held a *siddur*, a Jewish prayer book, in front of me. There were big, unknowable mysteries "out there" but here was a key to solving some of them. Two people were dead. I had already been attacked. This wasn't a game I was playing. But I felt I was on a path to solving a big, knowable mystery. My heart pumping hard, I started thumb-typing.

I sent a text to the same cell number I'd called earlier:

I'd like to talk to you tonight, alone.

I set down the phone and waited. It took less than a minute for Fly to send his reply:

Y?

I was ready for that. I was also aware that if he meant to harm me, he would need my phone if there were potentially incriminating texts on it. Rather than parcel it out, I hit him with the full blast:

Lippy played "More Coffee" in old Tippi film.
I have it.

I added a second message, the good cop to my own bad cop:

No Dickson. Just us. Just talk.

It took a little over a minute for Fly to write:

Where?

I told him to come to the deli. He wrote back:

U solo 2

I wasn't sure whether that was a question or a command. It didn't matter. I assured him I would be alone. He said he would be here in about a half-hour. I didn't bother asking him to park out front where I could see. He could always drop someone off down the street. There wasn't a lot of pedestrian traffic but there was enough. We'd sit in the dining room with the lights on. I would leave the door unlocked. If he tried to hurt me, someone would see or hear. But I didn't think he would. Not with my cell phone in a plastic bag stuck deep in one of four tubs of coleslaw. I made sure to leave the big pickle containers in full view on the prep table so he would have to go through those first. If he made me do it, brine in the eyes wouldn't be the most pleasant thing he'd ever experienced.

The wait was longer than a half-hour. As it came

up to nearly an hour, I was starting to feel as though I'd been had: that he wouldn't show or, less appealing, that he had stopped to pick up his posse and he'd show with thugs to strong-arm me into telling them where the phone was before poisoning me with my own tainted herring. I was actually considering calling Grant when a black Escalade pulled up. The windows were President of the United States-dark and, as the damn thing just sat there, I wouldn't have known whether it was Fly waiting to make sure we were alone or four armed killers. Even after the music mogul cracked the driver's side door of the Cadillac SUV and stepped out, I had no way of knowing whether he was alone. He stepped around the front of the big vehicle looking up and down the street—and not for traffic. He came around the car looking different than usual: he was dressed in blue jeans, a button-down long-sleeve white shirt—tails untucked—and a pair of Nike Dunks, which are over two grand a pair. I know that because Dani was always saying to Luke how she wished she could buy him a pair but couldn't on her salary. That topic always seemed to come up when the lovebirds were around me. The last time she said it, I told her I couldn't afford the footwear on my salary, either. Though it was dark, Fly was wearing the obligatory sunglasses. They were Luxuriator with white gold frames and cut diamonds on the hinges.

He wasn't wearing his ear-buds. That was a first.

Fly came to the door with purpose and confidence, a man who was unaccustomed to being barred from any club, any woman's door.

He saw me and came over without hesitation, sat without ceremony or acknowledgement, folded his ringed fingers in front of him, and peered at me through those opaque lenses.

"Sorry I'm late," he said affably. "Sunday night construction on Twenty-four."

And down the drain went another stereotype.

"It's okay," I said. "Want anything?"

"Where's your water at?" he asked.

"Ice?"

"Yeah. Please."

I went and got some. This was as chastened a Fly as I had ever seen, but I still wasn't convinced it wasn't an act. And I wasn't sure whether that made me smart or pitiful.

Neither, I told myself. *Just cautious.* Regardless, I never took my eyes from the table, watching it in the mirror above the counter or peripherally or directly.

"My Hire says I shouldn't talk to you," he said as I returned.

"Your—?"

"My Hire. My Liar Hire. My legal."

"Ah. So why are you?"

"'Cause I gotta tell someone who I'm not payin'," he said. "Or who isn't payin' me."

"Mr. Strong wasn't too happy having this on his shoe, was he?"

"You know that," Fly said, looking over his sunglasses. "But you were here, you saw me—I didn't go anywhere near him."

I wanted to tell him I hadn't exactly been paying attention, but I didn't think that was a good idea. Based on his deferential manner, my guess was he came here looking for an ally in case he moved from being a potential person-of-interest to a person-on-trial-for-murder.

"So why are we here?" I asked. "What *did* you do?"

He was still looking at me. "You not wearin' a wire?" He shook the salt shaker from side to side. "Ain't no bug in here?"

"No to both," I replied. "Trust me, Fly. I didn't call Grant. If I thought you were a killer, I wouldn't be here alone with you."

He considered that. "All true, all true."

"But wouldn't doing time be a good thing?" I couldn't help but ask. "Give some weight to your street cred?"

"Girl, you are so not-street," he said. "That's for rappers. Ducers like me—uh-uh."

"Ducers?"

"*Pro*ducers," he said, clearly annoyed that he was going to have to speak something like traditional English with me.

He sat back, hid behind his glasses again, continued to move the salt shaker back and forth. He was apparently thinking about how to confess whatever he wanted to confess.

"I truly did not realize what I had done," Fly said with uncharacteristic introspection and—it wasn't so much fear as . . . humility? "I woke up with this song in my head. I hummed it into my recorder and went back to sleep. I woke up and took it to the studio where I developed it with my crew. I didn't realize until—jeez, it was five or six months later, when I heard it again, that I realized *where* I heard it."

"On the street corner," I said with sudden realization.

"On the street corner," he said quietly. "I didn't say anything about it. I should have but I didn't. A couple months after that, when Lippy heard 'More Coffee,' he checked it out online and came to the same conclusion you did—that I was part of De F Chicken."

"Did you try to make it good with him?"

"I did. We met here, in fact. He showed me this crib sheet where he wrote out his melodies. Okay, I figured he could've forged that. Then he told me about the movie he'd made with his sister and how the song was in it."

"You checked?"

"What do you think?"

"Just making sure," I said.

He shook his head at the memory. "I tried to fix this even though talkin' to that boy was like talkin' to a pancake. I explained nice an' slow that I could give him *money* right away, but I couldn't put his name on the song. I said I could make him part of De F Chicken and he could work with us on the next things we did, share in the creative process, but he could not, must not *ever* tell anyone about our little deal. Our friend wasn't happy with that but he didn't reject it. At least, not outright."

"How long was that before he was poisoned?"

"Two, three weeks. He said he had to talk to his sister about it first."

"But according to her, he didn't," I said. "Not really. He just told her there was 'something' brewing."

"I know," Fly said. "I think it was a stall. He wanted to get credit for 'More Coffee.' Every time he heard it, he said it was like a knife in his ears."

"You can understand that, can't you?"

"Yeah, sure, but he was still being unreasonable," Fly said. "We talked again in my car. He said he wanted to record his own stuff, not with De F Chicken, and I told him okay but to slow down. That was when he just started backin' off the whole deal. He said he could probably get more money, more attention, if he just went to some dinowhore like Candy Sommerton and announced that he wrote this big hit song—even though a big part of its success was the arrangement, not anything that he did."

"Dinowhore?" I said, half in horror, half in admiration.

Fly didn't seem to hear me. He was somewhere between angry and scared.

"Lippy didn't seem to have much of a business sense," I said. "What do you think put that idea in his head?"

"He was just—I don't the hell know. Fed up? Tired of living a life on the edge of nowhere? Suddenly feeling like an artist who shouldn't compromise? All of that?"

"And maybe wanting to get his sister out of her business," I thought aloud.

"Porn?"

"No. She is an escort in Atlanta."

"A ho-bag? Man, I can see how that might have pushed Lippy."

"So getting back to this crib sheet—You figured if you could get that from the trumpet case, no one was likely to hear it in the movie."

"I saw him go down and I knew where it was. I just wanted to pull the damn thing out, put the case back, and leave. But the uber chav pasted it in there."

"Uber chav?"

"Dude thinks he bigger and smarter than he is," Fly said with disinterest.

"He messed you up," I pointed out.

"With kindergarten paste, jack. That's not cool."

"Neither is stealing a dead man's property," I pointed out. "Do you still have it?"

He shook his head slowly.

"But Strong knows because Detective Daniels traced the case to you forensically."

He nodded slowly.

"But you're in the clear, legally, as long as there isn't some distant relative who comes calling," I said. "No estate, no trial. No trial, no theft."

"Guilt without guilty," he said. "I ain't proud of what happened with the tune, but it was an accident I tried to fix. And the major talking point here is I ain't no killa."

I believed him. His story fit the facts from top to bottom, including why Lippy was so huggy toward the trumpet case on the morning he was killed.

A short silence followed. It felt like the moments after the last out in a losing ball game, when the stress kind of wafts away leaving a hole. I didn't know where to turn for a next step.

"You got a 'game over' face," he said.

"Funny. I was just thinking that."

"Yeah, well, I can't bow out," Fly said. "You know anything that I don't? That can help me?"

"Not much," I said.

"You know who else was here, the regulars?" he said. "I don't."

I told him who was here. He didn't know any of them except for Mad.

"You got a sense about any of 'em?" he asked.

I shook my head. "There doesn't seem to be any connection anywhere. Even Barron, who's an unscrupulous *schmuck*, doesn't have a role here."

"You sure Tippi got to town when she said she did?" he asked.

I frowned, hard. "That's harsh."

"Sibling rivalry. Wouldn't be the first time."

"I don't see it. And then what did she do, poison herself?"

"A partner-in-crime could've," he suggested. "Maybe there was an insurance policy or an inheritance from parents."

"I really don't think so," I said. I wasn't close to being anything like an honest-to-goodness profiler, but I knew women and I knew shock and awe in their eyes. Tippi was a lady in pain, not necessarily from Lippy but from life. The demands of her profession were there, of having to smile while she did God-knew-what to God-knew-who. If she was gunpowder, she would have blown at some john or film producer. Anyway, what could Lippy have had that he wouldn't have given her freely?

I told Fly I'd think about the various players and let him and Dickson know if anything occurred to me. I thanked him for coming.

He touched his fist to his heart. "I don't like being muscled, but I appreciate that you came to me and not the fuzz."

We both smiled. I was still half waiting for him to drop a shiv from his sleeve or pull a zip gun from his pocket, or for the other peeps of De F Chicken to pour from the Caddy. It both pleased and relieved me when he pulled from the curb without a spray of fire from an AK-47.

I sat there in the silent deli, cocooned by darkness and realizing that I had practically nothing to go on now. If not Fly, then who did kill Lippy and Tippi? And, just as perplexing, why?

Chapter 24

Speaking of the dinowhore—a description that both offended me and made me chuckle, a schizophrenic combination—Candy Sommerton was waiting for me when I arrived at the courtroom, nine forty-five on Monday morning.

"Ms. Katz, how do you think you're going to do in there?" she asked.

We were on the lower steps. I kept walking. Candy was hovering close behind her microphone while her camera operator hovered close behind her, both of them undulating as we made our way up the stairs. They reminded me of one of those Chinese New Year's dragons, complete with the big eyes and protruding tongue.

"I think it'll either go for me or against me," I said.

Candy was unfazed. Either sarcasm was lost on

her or she was bulldog enough to want a useful sound bite. Probably both.

"Do you feel your actions are impeding the educational growth of our young or standing up for religious freedom?" she pressed.

"Neither," I replied icily.

"How can you say that when you're denying students access to a historical site while allowing witches to worship there?"

She succeeded in pissing me off. I knew I shouldn't, but I stopped.

"That's not a question, it's an accusation."

"Are you saying it doesn't apply?"

"I'm saying you're a dino*meeskite*," I said, and walked on. Normally I'm not one for name calling, but she really didn't leave me another exit.

As I entered the security area, I saw that Reynold Sterne was in line, looking concerned and self-important, standing right behind Andrew Dickson III, who looked composed and self-important. They both gave me the briefest glance as they emptied their pockets and went through the metal detector. By the time I got inside, they were seated in the gallery. Joseph Bushyhead was already present.

The judge entered promptly at ten and our "matter" was called by the clerk.

"I've read the relevant police and medical accounts of the assault on Ms. Katz, and have decided that until the police investigation into this matter is completed there will be neither a university or Wiccan presence on the property."

That drew instant objections from both attorneys. The judge was ready for them; she whammed her gavel once, hard.

"The security of our citizens must take precedence over any other consideration, and as we do not know whether either of these parties or some third party was responsible for the home invasion and attack, until the picture is clearer, this order will be in effect."

"Your Honor, may a representative of the university address the court?" Dickson asked.

"There is no point, since the order has been given and recorded."

"But Your Honor, the ruling taints by association the spotless record of a highly regarded institution—"

"Which, I see, hired a criminally charged mixed martial artist as a security guard for the property and did not directly disclose to the victim in this matter that it possessed a key to her home. Does the statement address these questionable actions?"

"We did not know they would be presented for rebuttal."

"Then you may rebut them one week from today when we reconvene on this matter," she said. The gavel came down again. The next case was called.

It wasn't a total victory for me, but it was definitely a setback for everyone else. A week without trespassers suddenly seemed like the greatest gift in the world. It didn't mean that whoever blew toxins in my face wouldn't be back, but it's an imperfect world. Hopefully, that threat wouldn't linger much longer.

I managed to avoid Candy Sommerton by waiting until Dickson had left. I had a feeling he'd go right for the camera to *kvetch* about the order. I hurried away, arriving at the deli just in time to help with the lunch rush. I still hadn't decided what to do about Fly and the trumpet case, whether or not to tell Grant. There didn't seem any reason to. Plus, I had promised Fly.

Thom was giddy with delight when I told her what had happened in court. Obviously, it wasn't just my good news but Dickson's bad news that pleased her. I already knew what my daily observation would be: that for some people, ecstasy is expressed by clucking like a *grogger*, a Purim noise-maker.

To my surprise—and to the surprise of the staff—the deli was packed. It was as if a bus giving tours of all the Jewish establishments in Tennessee had parked on my street. Only as the diners took their seats did I realize who—and what—it was.

They were students. And they were only ordering coffee. When that was finished, they ordered—ironically—more coffee, which is free. They just sat and drank and talked and texted and iPadded for an hour, forcing regular customers or actual tourists to go elsewhere. It was like Occupy Wall Street, but with an IQ.

"What's going on?" Thom asked after the first round of coffees.

"I'm guessing Reynold Sterne had this ready to go," I said. "When the ruling went against them, he had his university students ready to thank me."

"And we will do this, like, every day," said a short, plucky thing with stringy hair, critical eyes, thrift shop clothes, and a voice that twittered from somewhere in her nasal cavity. "It's called civil disobedience."

"Actually, it's called a sit-in," I said, "only with a cup of joe. And despite what *Dr.* Sterne may have told you, this will not be a daily occurrence. New store policy: refills are not free. Next new store policy: starting tomorrow, there will be a sign announcing a thirty minute limit during prime dining hours. Enjoy your java—what's your name?"

"Kamala Moon."

"Right. Sterne mentioned you. Your future depends on your digging up my basement."

"It's larger than that," she said, standing her ground. "The advancement of knowledge depends on defeating inquisitors like you. We will find other ways to express ourselves."

"And other places," I said.

"You little brat!" Thom finally jumped in, her good humor having burned away.

"She's not a brat," I said. "She's part of a generation that was never taught 'no.' She's the result of a political mindset that told her she's entitled to take from *me* because she's a student with no money. But if she knows her history—and I hope she does, being educated and all, I hope she realizes that her kind always loses. They lose because you can't build anything by stealing bricks, occupying the site, or damning the landlord. You want to hurt me? Open a deli across the street." I came closer to that stern, unforgiving face. "But that takes effort, not just a short-term snit or an easy condemnation."

"You don't know me well enough to call me names!" She shouted that, silencing the other voices in the deli. "We want to work! We want to learn! You're the one who's stopping us!"

"I'm not stopping anything," I said. "You want to dig in my den?"

"We want what we were promised."

"Well, kid, life threw you a *legal* curve," I said. "Nothing is guaranteed. I asked you a question."

She took a moment to replay it in her angry little brain. "Yes. We want to dig, to expand our understanding of—"

"Then stop *hockin me a chinick*," I told her. "Buy the damn place, tear it down, do whatever the hell you want. *That* gets you access. *This* gets you nothing."

"But we may not find anything!" a voice said from one of the tables. I turned to look at a young white man with dreadlocks and the best urbanwear daddy's credit card could buy. "We need to know that."

"*Boychik*," I said, "you pays your money and you takes your chances."

"Amen," Thom said.

Kamala Moon's sneer was instantaneous and audible. "That's *your* take, old lady." Her eyes rolled to Thom. "Old *ladies*." She looked back at me. "You talk about entitlement but, like, you need to make a profit or you won't help us. That's part of the past, too. We know about it and we don't accept it." She moved in closer now. We were practically eye-to—well, my chin. "We will dig there, I promise. One way or another, education will defeat your greed."

And then I saw it. Her height about a forehead less than mine. A puff of toxin, a blur, and then me hitting the cold, weedy front lawn. She saw that I saw it and she smiled.

The young woman, with ice in her lips, leaned close to my ear and said, "Prove it."

I don't know what chilled me more, the act she had committed or the confident, unremorseful, cold-bloodedness with which she took ownership of it.

I stepped back. I smiled. "Not a problem."

"Liar," she replied, remaining stoic as you please.

I turned to the student with the dreadlocks. "Tell you what. Let's see who has the courage of their convictions. Your archaeological team can have free access to my den. Come and go whenever you want for as long as you want."

"What's the catch?" the young man asked.

"I love it," I said. "I'm supposed to give freely but it's a 'catch' when I ask for something from you. Here it is: I want spit. From each of you."

The dining room was even quieter than before. The few patrons who were not students were riveted, like they were in the audience of Court TV.

"Like, what are you even *talking* about?" Kamala Moon asked.

"The NPD pulled some DNA from my boiler room," I said. "That's where the intruder was on the night I was attacked." I paused. "I'm sure all of you know my home was invaded and I was assaulted. Or didn't your ringleader tell you that?"

There was a low murmur. Obviously, the covert action had been need-to-know.

"I think it was a pair of students who had access to my door key and I want to know who they were," I went on. "Those two individuals will probably spend the first year of the dig in prison for criminal trespass and aggravated assault . . . but your sacrifice will give the rest of the students access to a potentially valuable historical site." I looked around at two dozen or so blank young faces that gave me very little hope for the future. I stopped on the pale face surrounded by knotted braids. "So? Do we have a deal? Everyone spit into a cup and you can start jackhammering tonight."

There were a few "sures" and "yeahs" and a couple of "is that legals" but only granite silence from Dreadlock Boy and Belladonna Girl.

I turned back to the little *moisheh kapoyer* sitting at the table. He was the weak link. He was probably the dope who went downstairs and pretended to be a Civil War laborer.

"You look like you want to spit," I said. I plucked a napkin from a holder and turned my cheek toward him. "Go ahead. Right there. Unless you've got something to hide. In which case, with all these witnesses testifying that you refused, the court can demand it."

"Don't spit—because you're not an animal!" Kamala told him.

"That's right," the young man said to me. "I'm not."

"No," I said. "Just a coward who won't own up to his actions." I gave him another few seconds. He looked away. I turned back to the ringleader. "How about you?"

She hesitated. "I'll give you my spit."

I moved in so the others couldn't hear. "Because you weren't inside my house. You didn't perspire on my floor. You just blew poison in my face. You don't get charged unless your buddy cracks and rats when they pin this on him. And they will. So here's the deal. You do a quick about-face with the prof. You and your friends. You find other projects for your theses. You convince him to leave me alone. Maybe—*maybe*—he and I can work something out without a gun to our heads . . . or belladonna in our faces. Do that or do time."

Watching Kamala Moon was like watching a blowfish . . . deflate. Now that she had something to lose, she wasn't so interested in manning the barricades. And maybe there was something else at work, the revelation that there was another way to do this. Not by making demands but by making conversation. If college taught her nothing but that, it would be worth the time and expense.

"You promise to talk to Dr. Sterne?" she asked, some of her belligerence returning—for show, I imagined.

"I said I would. Don't push me."

"You're pushing me."

"I'm thinking those should be your last words before you go," I said.

Young Kamala Moon, the self-appointed voice of her generation, hesitated—then grabbed her bag and turned to go. Thom was standing in front of her, between tables, so she couldn't go around.

"That'll be a buck from everyone," Thom said in a loud voice. "And a tip would be greatly appreciated by your waitstaff."

Kamala Moon fished a crumpled dollar from her back pocket. Bills and coins hit the tables like pennies from heaven as the kids didn't wait for the checks but left. When the door had clapped shut behind the last of the powdered *tuchases*, Luke came from the kitchen and hugged me.

"You were awesome," he said.

There were nods from the remaining patrons and proud smiles from the staff. I grinned tightly then went to my office to *plotz*. The whole thing was kind of a blur, and I think I was mostly bluffing, but at least the second of the mysteries was cleared up.

I knew who took the trumpet case.

I knew who tried to poison me.

Now all that remained was the eight hundred pound *behemot* in the room: who killed Lippy and Tippi?

Chapter 25

It was strange to be checking off solutions without sharing them with Grant. Not strange in a personal context, just in a procedural sense. In the few cases that had fallen in my lap since Hoppy Hopewell literally fell in my lap, he was always a part. That's how we hooked up, turning brainstorming into a sleepover.

It felt good to be flying solo in that regard as well. It was narcotic, lifting me from the quasi-depression that I was in. I blew through the rest of the day on adrenaline, and when I went home, I was ready to sleep. The lawn was clear of Wiccans and their tent, the street was clear of what may or may not have been Dickson watching me from a car, and I didn't smell anything that hinted of an unwashed mass. I knew I was safe because my cats came to the door to let me know they were hungry.

I felt a twinge of guilt as I cranked open two

cans of cat food. The way I thought about the students *did* cause me to face the fact that my disappointment with the young and with Dickson was turning me into something of a reactionary. I had seen that happen with my uncles and with senior investment people. I had never liked it in them and I didn't like it in me—though apart from this little pang, I didn't throw up any sandbags. They had caused it. That's why the word was "reactionary." And there was—of course—a Yiddish phrase which took on that inevitability: *An ofter gast falt tsu last.*

A frequent guest becomes a burden.

Throughout my adult life I've listened, I've listened some more, I've given to charity, I've given my trust, and all I hear is the same thing: give me what you worked hard to have. Not just my assets but my self-respect. My freedom. So I've moved to the right where I don't have to hear. I've backed away from men so I don't have to be disappointed.

Who's at fault?

I had brought home split pea soup, and while I warmed it and heated a few slices of *challah*, I went to the laptop on the coffee table and checked e-mail and Facebook. There was nothing pressing, nothing especially interesting. Facebook had too many obscure posts with people asking what they meant, or self-pitying laments with friends offering the expected buck-up replies. It was a waste of tired eyeballs. Even the photos, which took too long to load, showed more and more people who I knew less and less about. Allie Mihalko, who I had worked with in New York, had a husband and he had a family. My Manhattan neighbors had puppies; I was glad I wasn't there to hear them bark.

Vei is mir, I thought. The world is growing utterly narcissistic and you are going completely sour.

Thinking of the world made me wonder if the earth was happy, now that it wasn't going to be forced to share its bounty with the university. I went ahead and looked to see if there was a Facebook page for the Nashville Coven. There was for everything else. I hadn't bothered to look before because, honestly, I'd had enough of Wiccans right from the start. Now was the time to do the whole "keep your enemies closer" thing.

I found it and was surprised to find someone I didn't know post about this being the fifth anniversary of their entry into the coven. There were, as was to be expected, a battery of "likes" and a flurry of congratulatory replies.

There was something else. More of the same.

I got my soup and sat by the computer with it and researched Wiccan anniversaries. They were referred to as Days of the *Propicius Spīritus.* I looked it up. The phrase was a merging of English, Middle English, and Latin—symbolically, a stretching-across-time—and it meant, not unexpectedly, days of propitious spirits. Meaning that it was a good time to act.

"Act on what?" I wondered.

Further reading revealed the expected: It was a good time to act to honor whatever you were celebrating. But it was also a good time to act against whatever bad may have occurred on that date.

I looked back to the day Lippy was killed; no one had posted anything about any anniversary. So that was a dead end.

And then it was *Whoa Nellie!* as Bozo the Clown used to shout on TV when I was a very little girl. What I saw was like a thunderclap, scary but illuminating. I looked up *Come Blow Your Horny* on the tongue-twisting site, AFCACDB. Damn—the answer was there. *Right there.* I looked up a celebrity home on Google Map, then checked the online archive of the *Nashville National.* I had an all-access password thanks to a debt owed me by the owner, Robert Reid. I went back ten years— and *bingo!* again. Both were a perfect fit. I looked up Bill "Spud" Carla's online store, checked the list of vitamins and supplements he offered for sale. I clicked on several of them to see what they did. I found what I was looking for as I finished my soup.

It all made sense. Sick, vengeful, nasty sense.

I checked an address in the online white pages, then grabbed my bag and got in the car.

I had no idea exactly where I was going, so I plugged the address into my cell phone GPS. When that was set I made a call. What was about to happen would not be pretty, however it went. If it was at all possible, I wanted to make sure it wouldn't also be deadly.

But this thing was also mine. I didn't want Grant Daniels involved in this. He would probably think I was nuts. If I was, no one would know but me. Besides, if he showed up, there was no guarantee that things would go the way they needed to.

There were no Native American reservations in Tennessee. The state did, however, have a Native American Indian Association, which oversaw small communities and apartment buildings that provided housing and assistance for persons of Native American descent. For the Cherokee in Davidson County, that was an older housing development in the Bordeaux-Whites Creek area west of the city. Bordered generally by the Cumberland River, I-24, and the county line, the region is mostly rural and hilly with occasional pockets of tract houses fifty and sixty years old and trailer homes which only looked that old. Frank James, the notorious brother of outlaw Jesse, lived here for many years.

The perfect place for a criminal to hide, I thought as I left the highway and made my way along dark, untraveled Whites Creek Pike.

I probably should have waited until the daytime, but I wouldn't have been able to sleep. Not with this new idea bubbling in my brain.

Better to be dead? I asked myself.

Not if I did this right. And that was it, wasn't it? I wanted this challenge. I created it, I invoked it. I had pushed myself and, so doing, I had cleared my property of squatters and found out who had attacked me. *I* did that, without Grant, without an attorney. I liked feeling *something*, even if it was dangerous—including fear over the possibility of being force-fed daphne or some other unhappy herb.

I had the window open. I could literally smell the change of scenery from my tree-lined street with the clinging scent of gas fumes and neighborhood cooking to—how had A.J. once put it? "To where the Cumberland Plateau just wears out." The Appalachians were to the east and they sloped down to where I was now, a world of old growth trees like eastern hemlocks—isn't that what Socrates drank to depart Ancient Greece?—northern red oaks, and American chestnuts. It was like a salad bar in a health food store. I loved the sizzling grill at the deli, but that only went as far as the nose. There was no doubt that this air got into your cells and did a Snoopy dance.

It was almost anesthetizing and I had to focus to stay alert—especially with a road where there was more likelihood of hitting a bear than another vehicle.

The thirty-acre spread of low-lying homes—cottages, really—came up on the right. I got off the highway and followed the curving exit to the north. The Cherokee Nation Village was announced by a weather-worn wooden sign planted in the ground. An old post stood behind and above it with a red-and-white PRIVATE PROPERTY sign—peppered with rusted dents from what looked like target practice with a BB gun. The pulsing dot on my cell phone told me to follow Whites Creek Annex—a big C-shaped road—to near the end. Sally Biglake lived on a small, dead-end street named Coventree.

Of course.

I knew the witch would be in because the Facebook page said she was holding a meeting at her home. I was guessing their banishment was on the agenda. I had every right to be there, I supposed, though I had no idea whether I would be welcome. That I would be admitted, I did not doubt, not after I said what I had to say.

Sally's home was at the end of a cul-de-sac. Illuminated by a single yellow lantern above the front door, the cottage was an adorable log cabin. There was a rainbow spray of all kinds of plants in hanging pots and window boxes, in the garden along the entire front and in the windows. The driveway was to the left, a vegetable garden was fenced off to the right. The nearest neighbors were about two acres behind me on both sides of the street. Sally's motorcycle was there, along with a van, a Volvo, and a vintage Volkswagen love bug.

I killed the headlights as I neared and pulled to the curb well before the cottage. I exited quietly and took several long, deep swallows of rustic air. My heart was thudding so hard it actually scared me; I didn't know hearts could do that without *plotzing*.

I started toward the cottage, my shoes crunching on dirt that had washed down onto the old asphalt road. Apart from crickets, owls, and an occasional dog bark, it was the only sound. I looked up. The stars were brighter here than in Nashville. I smiled as I flashed back to being at the Hayden Planetarium as a sixth grader. It had been fan cooled, like the air felt now. My heart was thumping then because I had loitered and maneuvered going in so I would be next to Hershel Lewis. I'd had a crush on him. He was a tall, quiet kid who was also the president of the audio-visual club. I'd admired how sure he was of his equipment. His projectors and record players, I mean. He had a ring of school keys hooked to his belt and stuffed in his pocket and whenever he had to leave class there were no questions asked.

Maybe I was spoiled at a young age to be drawn to men who had confidence and suction with the powers-that-be. My husband had been like that. And Grant. And the crush I had felt on that bum-lord Stephen R. Hatfield, who treated his tenants and his women like crap, but, boy, did he have confidence and local pull.

Get over that shmontses, I told myself. *It was understandable when you were twelve. It isn't now.*

I was at the front door. Beating myself up had slowed my heart rate. The cat that had gone rat-catching at my house was circling my feet and mewing. I didn't need to ring the doorbell—which, I noticed now, did not exist. Sally opened the door. She was dressed in a white robe with red floral patterns on the sleeves—roses and thorns. She looked at me with a rocky jaw, all solid lines and lumps. It softened quickly.

"Sister Gwen," she said. "It's so good to see you! You were the one most hoped for yet the last anticipated."

"I'm sure," I said. "I mean, after all the hubbub about the temple."

"All in the past now." She pivoted away like Ali Baba's stone wall swinging wide. "Please. Join us."

Chapter 26

I walked into Sally's cottage, which was apparently one large room with a kitchen and bedroom, front and back, respectively. The smell of hickory was strong. It was coming from a smoking, woklike affair in the center of the room. The ladies were seated in a circle around it, on a red rug with a white pentagram stitched in the center. The smoke got into one's nostrils but the open windows kept it from becoming suffocating.

The "us" was everyone. Mad was there along with Ginnifer Boone, the palm reader from New Orleans; Dalila Odinga, the voodoo gal from Kenya; and the four others, to whom I hadn't been introduced when they showed up at my home the night Reynold Sterne was there. Sally told me the names of the other women but I promptly forgot them. My heart was tap dancing again and I needed to calm myself.

I couldn't read the other women. I felt as if I'd interrupted something and they were simply on pause. At a gesture from Sally, they tightened the circle to make room for me.

"You saved us the bother of summoning you," Sally said amiably. It didn't sound as friendly as she made it seem.

"You could have just phoned," I said, taking my place between Mad and Ginnifer. Sally sat across from us.

"A compulsion spell is different," the coven leader said.

"What is it, like an astral kidnapping?"

"Oh, it's hardly that. An abduction would be barbaric." Her smile, which had been constant, faded a little at the edges. "You do understand that there's a difference between barbarism and Druidism."

"If you say so," I said. "But there's something that interests me more than that."

"What would that be?" Sally asked.

"First, this thing about the earth not being happy." I looked at Mad. "My, uh—my sister said that several times at the deli. I assumed it meant that the digging up of the campsite on my property, disturbing any old bones, was what she was referring to. Why else tell me? Nothing else I was doing could have upset the earth, as far as I know."

"The earth is happy now," Mad said distantly, like a chant, to no one in particular.

"Right," I said. "But not because the temple or the order from the bench stopped the university from digging there. That had nothing at all to do with me, did it?"

"It did not," Sally acknowledged.

I hadn't had to pry that from her. She didn't try to change the subject. She just waited. I didn't think that boded well for me.

"It had to do with an anniversary," I went on. "According to the calendar on Facebook, first, fifth, tenth, and twenty-fifth are the big ones."

"We describe those as the 'perfect years,'" Sally explained. "Astrological alignments recur, allowing a direct connection to what is called the spawning day."

"The day something happened, either good or bad," I said. "The day you can draw on or dispel the good or bad energies an event caused. Since the earth wasn't happy, I have to assume the anniversary was something not-so-good."

"Again, you're correct," Sally said. She seemed almost proud that her newly minted sister was so quick on the uptake.

"I thought back to something one of my workers told me last week," I said. I looked at Mad. "About a Cherokee jeweler named Jim Pinegoose you were going to marry in 2003. Ten years ago. Making this one of the 'perfect years.'"

Mad was staring ahead in silence, her eyes on the rising smoke of the smoldering hickory.

"Jim suffered heart failure during a tribal competition dance. Last week you tried to get in touch with him through some kind of tribal ceremony."

"*Atskili*," Sally said.

"Right. In the woods behind Barbara Mandrell's home. That was where you held the tribal dance, wasn't it?"

Sally was positively beaming. "It was. So . . . you understand!"

I smiled. "Completely. It was the dancing that killed him, but not really. His heart had been weakened by a natural drug that someone had been giving him. Potassium, I'm guessing, since enough of that can lead to a heart attack during unusual exertion. Since he was Cherokee, the medical examiner would have accepted the finding of the tribal doctor, who wouldn't have bothered to look for a chemical imbalance in a man who died while dancing wildly."

Mad's breathing had gone shallow. Her tattooed teeth were rolling as she ground her real teeth.

I turned to the older woman. "Jim Pinegoose was having an affair, wasn't he?"

"No!" Mad snapped without looking at me.

I smiled. "I looked up the newspaper coverage of your powwow. All kinds of wares were sold there, including his jewelry. Someone had bought his jewelry from a boutique in California. For a movie. She came to see the jeweler in person when she was here. He was smitten with her because, let's face it, the gal oozed sex appeal. She and Jim worked out an arrangement. More jewelry for sex. It wasn't really an affair, it was a business transaction."

"She was evil—"

"She was a kid who was doing the best she could in the only way she knew how," I said. "That 'barter' arrangement was consummated a few days before Jim's death—sometime between September third, when the powwow began, and September tenth, when he died during the closing ceremony. Enough time for him to be toxified. How did you find out?"

"He told me," Mad said. "He felt *possessed*."

"He felt guilty," I said.

The room was silent for a long moment. The only sound was the faint pop and crackle of the flame-heated hickory. Sally seemed delighted, the other women remained respectfully on alert, but Mad was practically hyperventilating.

I swiveled slightly toward Mad and inched closer. "You poisoned Lippy with mercury, at the deli, because it was the only way you knew to guarantee that his sister would come here the next day—September tenth," I went on. "You weren't even sure where she was, only that she had to be there on that day, the spawning day." I looked at Sally. "What would killing Tippi Montgomery on that day have done, spiritually speaking?"

"It would have cleansed Jim Pinegoose's soul," Sally said.

"It was not his fault!" Mad hissed. "It was that succubus! She lured him to a sinful union, brought bad energy into our lives!"

"And that cloud stayed with you until you killed her," I said.

"It hovered over the very earth on which we moved," Sally said. "It poisoned all of the sisters of the coven."

I looked around the circle. "So you all knew?"

"We all played parts," Sally confessed openly. "One obtained the elements, two watched the individuals, another helped to transport Mad, our offended sister, to and from the unhallowed spirit."

"You mean Tippi Montgomery? Your victim?"

"Call her by any name you like," Sally said. "The deed remains the deed."

"As does yours," I said. "Murder. That's a helluva lot more serious than what she may have done."

I made a move as if to get up, only to have Dalila grab my right arm. I turned to her—and from the corner of my eye I saw Sally lunge forward. I thought she was going to attack me but all I saw was an explosion of yellow smoke. It smelled like burnt spinach pie and it coated my mouth and nostrils in the single breath I took before I could stop myself—something the Wiccans had been prepared for. My head didn't swim, it flew, as though I'd taken a mega-hit of nitrous oxide. I was aware of a second burst, of green smoke—the counteragent, no doubt—as my body was maneuvered onto its back. Other than move my arms like weak turtle flippers, there was nothing I could do to fight back. I was on the rug looking up through tearing eyes at a purplish haze. I didn't know whether they were going to poison me or cut my heart out or feed me to the cat. All I knew was that I was glad I'd anticipated something like this.

K-Two charged through the front door as if she were entering a steel cage. I knew that because I heard her cry. I sucked in the rush of fresh air that came in with her. I felt myself pulled aside by the shoulders as legs and forearms and elbows and even a head protected the area above and around me. I heard grunts and cries. I heard the cat yowl as if it had been stepped on. I felt my lips move, though only my brain spoke:

How ya feelin' now, earth?

I was yanked again, dropped, there were more shouts and smacks, and then I was hefted upwards. My hazy mind pictured it like that scene in *Camelot*, when Lancelot rescues Guinevere from the burning stake . . . only without the girlish longing in my loins for Franco Nero. My head bobbled up and down as we rushed from the cabin into the darkness.

"Gwen, you okay?"

I said something that was intended to be "yes" but sounded to me like "whuuu."

"I got water in the truck," she said. "You'll be better in a sec."

I was bounced around a little more as she knocked down the tailgate of her pickup with an elbow and laid me down. The next thing I knew, bottled water was being dribbled into my mouth and rubbed on my face. It felt good, but mostly it was the fresh air that did it.

"You're lucky," K-Two was saying. "I just got here seconds before that juju exploded."

I didn't ask how she spelled that. I think I knew what she meant.

"You could've given me more notice," she went on. "I had to drive like crazy."

"Witches," I said. "What—what—"

"They ain't coming after us, if that's what you're asking. I knocked 'em around pretty good."

"Cell picture, phone in my pocket," I said. "Smoke."

It took a second before K-Two got what I meant. "Good idea. Evidence."

She left me, I heard her door slam, I saw her run toward the house, and then I lost her. When she came back, my head had cleared considerably.

"Got it," she said.

"I also used my cell to record what they said while I was in there," I said.

"Those crazies are toast," she said admiringly.

I did hope so. I would hate it if my savior got into trouble for pulling my *tuchas* from the fire.

By the time other residents of the block had noticed the fumes, I was well enough to get behind the wheel of my car and drive out with K-Two covering my retreat. No one stopped us and no one called the police. What happened on Cherokee land stayed on Cherokee land.

Happily, one of those happenings was not my demise.

It was eleven p.m. by the time I got home, loaded the recording and photographs onto my computer, and paid K-Two the two hundred bucks I had offered her to come out and play bodyguard.

She initially declined the fee, since she was pleased to be able to use her skills to actually help someone. But I insisted.

"You saved my life," I reminded her. "That's worth at least a pair of c-notes."

K-Two stayed to continue earning her money, just in case "those loony lucys," as she called them, returned—and also to back up my story for the police.

When I had showered and made some licorice tea—I needed an aroma in my nasal passages other than rotten vegetables—I called Grant at home. It sounded, from his initial *fumfitting*, like I'd interrupted something that wasn't a movie.

"I found out who killed Lippy and Tippi," I said, "because they almost just killed me."

He sounded skeptical. I told him what had transpired since I met with Fly Saucer the day before.

He told me he would be over to take a statement in a half-hour. I asked him to collect Detective Egan on the way so there wouldn't be any hurt feelings.

It was nearly midnight when the two detectives arrived in separate cars, although Egan was also accompanied by a squad car. We sat in my living room as I told them what had happened, and played them the recording.

Egan was dazzled. Grant was annoyed. I was tired.

Early in the meeting, Grant called and asked a couple of cars to go to Whites Creek Annex and check out the story. When we were nearly finished, they reported that the only one there was Sally Biglake, but that the neighbors had seen the others go.

I gave Grant the names of the Wiccans I remembered so they could be found and interviewed.

"Interviewed," I thought as he said the word. *It sounded so much gentler than "questioned" or "interrogated."* It was much more than a bunch of killers and their accomplices deserved.

Detective Egan talked to K-Two alone in the kitchen while Grant finished with me in the living room.

"I'm not happy with what you did," he said. "Withholding information and confronting a person of interest on your own."

"Would you have gone in and pinned their ears back?" I asked. "*Could* you have?"

"Eventually, yes," he said. "But the stuff about Fly . . . about the students. You could have told me."

"Promised I wouldn't," I said. "Not until I wrapped this up and they weren't in any real danger."

"For theft and assault," he said.

"A cover-your-rump miscalculation and a rookie error," I said. "I've made mistakes in my life, too."

"And paid for them."

We sat there without speaking. I was waiting. It wouldn't make any difference in our relationship, but what I wanted to hear would make all the difference in whether I talked to him again, ever.

"What you did was impressive, I do have to give you that," he said. "I had Fly in the crosshairs from the goatee hair, but not the students and certainly not Sally and her gang."

I smiled as I rolled the semi-validation over in my mind. "Thanks."

"You sure you don't want to go to the hospital for a once-over?" he asked. "You took a direct hit of what the officers think was hillbilly knock-out gas—what moonshiners used to use against the Feds."

"And that is?"

"Baked, powdered manure and urine."

As soon as he said that, I knew that I would never eat spinach again.

"'Manurine,'" I said. "Well, at least it was organic."

He looked at me, unsure whether or not I was joking. I wanted him to go home.

"I'm fine," I added. "What I need to do now is sleep until about Thursday."

"Well, I'll leave the cops behind until we've talked to the Wiccans, determined who might be a threat," Grant said. He shook his head. "That was crazy, you know that? Just—what's your word?"

Oh, my *word*.

"*Meshugenah*," I said patiently.

"Right. *Mishooguhnuh*. That's what it was."

It wasn't "my" word. It didn't belong to "you people." But I was too tired to educate him. I just smiled politely, with my eyes closed so I didn't have to look at him. I opened them in time to see him get up slowly, pushing off his knees like my father used to do. I saw the old man in Grant's future just then. The thought of being with one of those rigid, self-absorbed males brought back the smell of manurine.

Detective Egan had returned by now. She came over and shook my hand.

"That was really fine work," she beamed. "We should do lunch one day."

"Stop by the deli," I said. "It'll be my treat."

She smiled and her eyes lingered as she left. I couldn't tell if I'd just been complimented, hit on, or both. I didn't care.

It all felt good.

Chapter 27

The next morning, there was a new me looking back at myself from the mirror. She was proud, pleased, and relieved. She was eager to start the day.

I was up at my usual time feeling surprisingly rested. Losing a burden or two or three will do that, I guess. I did my morning routine, peeked out and saw the cops outside—along with Candy Sommerton's van, which did not surprise me—and resolved to start things fresh. Not fresh as in "give Grant another chance," but as in "stop trying to direct my life." I was going to take things as they came.

Candy hustled toward me, hauling her dragon-tail cameraman, as I walked to my car.

"Gwen—I know we haven't seen eye to eye on things, but you *have* to believe me: I want to tell this story. Your story. Is it true, what I read in the police report?"

I stopped and smiled at the camera. "I'll tell you what, Candy. Why don't you try this. Try not ambushing me for once. Come to the deli later, after lunch rush, and I'll talk to you then."

She jerked like a doll who'd just been wound up with a key. "Seriously?"

"Seriously."

"Exclusively?"

I made a face and held up my cell phone. There were over a dozen calls, three of them from Robert Reid at the *National*. One of them—the only voice mail I'd listened to—was from Reynold Sterne. He called to say that Kamala Moon had told him what she'd done and he wanted to tell me he was sorry. He said he wouldn't take any action until he talked to me but added that, going forward, they would take a much more sensitive approach to my needs; and they would not enforce the original agreement without my cooperation. That made me happy, too.

"I don't know who else wants to plaster me across the news," the new me told Candy, "but how about this: I promise I'll talk to you first."

"For real?"

I nodded.

Candy hesitated but quickly agreed. She had to

realize that calling this into the station would get her primo air time on the evening broadcast.

For the first time ever, she thanked me. We left as BFFs. That actually felt kind of good, too. It was better than wanting to tear off her head and stuff it like derma.

The cops stayed behind and I found another pair waiting for me at the deli. They were plain-clothes, sitting at a table, but Thom introduced them before giving me a big, shake-you-back-and-forth hug. Luke, Raylene, A.J., and Newt lined up like autograph-seekers on the red carpet to embrace me as well. We only had a half-hour to opening, a crowd was already starting to gather, and they knew better than to ask for details while there was work to be done.

Before we left the huddle, there was one thing I needed to say to them.

"This has been a week of anniversaries," I said. "One of them really, really good. The year that I've been here would have been godawful without all of you. I thank you all, I love you all, and I'm really looking forward to the next one."

We all had a good little cry through our smiles. Then I clapped twice and we went off to do our jobs.

There was one word I didn't tell them as I watched them go. I'm not sure they would have understood, not being any of "you people." But, then, it only mattered to me.

It was pride.

For the first time in my life, I, Gwen Katz, was *kvelling*.

Hilarious Mysteries from
Laura Levine

Available Wherever Books Are Sold!

All available as e-books, too!

Visit our website at **www.kensingtonbooks.com**